Blackstone's Fancy

Blackstone's Fancy

Richard Falkirk

STEIN AND DAY/*Publishers*/New York

First published in the United States by Stein and Day/*Publishers* 1973
Copyright © 1973 by Richard Falkirk
Library of Congress Catalog Card No. 73-80798
All rights reserved
Printed in the United States of America
Stein and Day/*Publishers*/7 East 48 Street, New York, N.Y. 10017
ISBN 0-8128-1604-8

AUTHOR'S NOTE

Research for the *Blackstone* series has been extensive. Of the many works of reference I have so far consulted I should like to acknowledge my particular debt to Kellow Chesney, who wrote *The Victorian Underworld*, a fine, painstaking book, which helped enormously in my exploration of the Regency underworld which spawned Mr. Chesney's criminals. And to John Ford who wrote *Prizefighting*, subtitled *The Age of Regency Boximania*, another excellent piece of exhaustive period research. In the interest of the narrative I have had to interfere very slightly with historical chronology and mood. My apologies to anyone whose sensibilities may be offended.

1

The old prizefighter patrolled the outer ring as if, once again, the spectators had assembled to see him. He had discarded his coat and the breeze flattened the silk of his white frilled shirt against his retired muscles, his disobedient belly. His nose had been spread by punches and there was a dent on the cheekbone beneath his left eye where bare knuckles had scored.

There were other ageing fighters circling the grass separating the inner ring from the crowd. And one or two younger ones in case the Fancy invaded as they had done when Scroggins fought Turner. But the old pugilist in the silk shirt was the foreman. His name was Hansom and he was reputed to have beaten Jem Belcher, although no one was specific about the date.

Blackstone watched him from a yellow-and-black postchaise fifty yards from the two rings, Irish-green and still sugared with frost this bright December lunch-time.

"Even now I wouldn't like to take him on," he said.

"I'd put my money on you," said Foley, the professional gambler.

"Then you'd lose."

"I don't think so." Foley neither countenanced nor acknowledged losses despite the decline of his home, his dress and his person. He was still handsomely dressed, but there was cracks in his tall boots, baldness on his green swallow-tail coat, jaundice on his high white collar. His face was long and saddened by the uncertainty of racing certainties, his cheeks brandy-flushed by erratic celebrations. But he was courtly and women liked him. "You see," he explained, "Hansom let himself go to seed." He uncrossed his legs, opening a crack in one boot like a mouth. "He drinks like a fish and eats like a horse. He should have taken a public house like some of the others. Cribb, Tom Belcher, Ned Painter, Tom Shelton. . . ."

"I still think I'd lose." Blackstone gazed over the tall hats of the ring-siders to the old fighter with the greying hair combed forward over a lumpy forehead. "He looks fit enough to me. Considering he's over forty."

"And you're?"

"Thirty," Blackstone said. "Or thereabouts."

"And fit?"

"Fairly." Blackstone tucked away his snuff-box.

"*And* you did a bit of milling yourself, didn't you?"

"Once upon a time. Before I joined the forces of law and order."

"And I should think you were quite good at it." Foley, who would lay odds on the sun rising and setting, appraised the power in Blackstone's shoulders. "Six to four you thrash Hansom."

"You're not that sure then."

"There's only two of you. A good price I should have thought. What about the odds today? The Gasman can't lose but the bookies are only offering five to four."

"How much have you wagered?"

8

"A hundred."

"A lot of money."

Foley shrugged, over-acting a little.

"You bet too heavily," Blackstone told him. They had been cricketing, racing and prizefighting friends of years—Lord's, Epsom Downs, the Daffy Club. Foley also followed cock-fighting, bull-baiting, and dog-fighting: Blackstone would have none of these.

"And you, Blackie? Haven't you made a wager?"

Blackstone nodded. "Ten pounds on the Gasman."

"And you a Bow Street Runner."

"What of it?"

"You're supposed to break up a prizefight, not support it." He lay back on the satin seat, dented hat tilted over his forehead, and regarded Blackstone slyly. "After all, it's illegal, isn't it? Under an Act of 1750 if I'm not mistaken." Foley was never mistaken about figures, only forecasts.

Blackstone said, "I'm looking for contacts, informants, witnesses." He grinned and took some snuff to disperse the lie.

Across the tops of the hats, as close together as roof tiles, John Hansom, or Handsome Jack as he'd been known in his brawling heyday, was tackling two intruders in the outer ring where, later, referee, umpires, backers and their friends would take their places. He waved aside the other fighters and put up his fists in classic stance. The two intruders, young and whippy, circled him warily: a couple of saplings beside a battered oak.

The Fancy—some had traveled sixty-six miles from London to Hungerford for the fight between Tom (Gasman) Hickman and Bill Neat—shouted encouragement to the old fighter.

"Tap some of their claret for them, me Handsome. Give 'em one of your old rib-roasters."

Foley said, "I'll give you six to four that Hansom puts them both down within three minutes."

Blackstone said, "Do you ever give any other odds?"

Beneath the white silk of his shirt you could see Hansom's biceps bunching. But they were no longer as pugnacious as their owner. However, you couldn't take away his experience.

One of the youths forgot the experience, prematurely heard the applause of his cockney friends and the sighs of the village girls they had met the night before. He ducked straight into a scarred, Sunday-joint of a fist and fell to the grass, blood oozing from his nostrils.

The Fancy were delighted. "Go it, Handsome. The first drop of claret to Handsome Jack. Now rattle the other culley's ivories for him."

The other fighters led the first youth away and Handsome Jack, who was far from handsome, turned to the second boy. The boy looked vulnerable now that his forces had been decimated.

Blackstone said, "He should let the poor little bastard go. It was only bravado."

Foley took out a hip-flask. "Perhaps. But that would only humiliate the lad. One punch, perhaps."

"Maybe. But I don't like the look of Handsome Jack."

"He was good in his day."

"I don't give a damn how good he was. There's something cruel about him."

"You don't expect him to look poetic, do you?"

The youth, wearing mud-spattered trousers strapped under his shoes, too big, as if they had belonged to his father, glanced at the crowd in search of support and attempted a smile. No support, the smile a mess.

And more of a mess as Hansom's right caught him full in the face.

The boy staggered and spat out a tooth.

Blackstone leaned forward, fists clenched. "The bastard! He didn't have to hit him as hard as that."

Foley agreed, swallowing a mouthful of brandy.

The crowd's shouts scattered until only a few were left. "That'll teach him, my Handsome. Now let him be."

The youth's fists, which had shrunk, were still up, but wavering. Hansom knocked them aside with his left and caught the boy on the cheek with his right. And then another left into the belly.

The other fighters caught the folding body and dragged it away. Hansom put his fists on his hips and posed before remembering to recall his belly, forgotten in his triumph.

Blackstone said, "I've a good mind to take him on. Who finally beat him when he was fighting? I'll give him a medal."

"Molyneux, The Black," Foley told him. "He should have been champion. He came from America to take the title from Cribb. But they reckon the cold beat him. The cold and a little cheating by Cribb's seconds."

"A medal for Molyneux then. Although he's dead, isn't he?"

Foley nodded. "Three years ago. The booze finished him," he added, stroking his flask thoughtfully. "They say Hansom still wants to fight every sambo he sees. Funny, isn't it, with the blacks being so popular. They also gave Molyneux the nickname of Snowball," Foley recalled. "Poor old Snowball, melting like that." He drank some brandy.

Blackstone looked at his gold Breguet watch, given to

11

him by a wealthy woman whose jewelry he had retrieved. "Another half-hour before they come up to the scratch," he said.

The sky was still a burnished blue but laced on the horizon with white clouds. The last of the Fancy were arriving on foot and horseback, in coaches and four, post-chaises and mails, horns sounding. Behind the swells, behind the carts, gigs and the carriages positioned over-night and the improvised stands, the crowd waited in the thin sunshine, supping porter and ale; eating hot pies; fighting; betting on cards, thimbles and rat-faced fighting dogs. Countrymen in smocks, with iron on the soles of their boots, cockneys from the Rookeries in punished velveteen with handkerchiefs at the throat; dustmen, lamp-lighters, farmers, butchers, grooms, weavers, water-men; pick-pockets, mudlarks, magsmen, a murderer or two and a few hopeful bawds. Among the swells in their white box-coats were half a dozen Members of Parliament, some fringe Royalty and a couple of furtive magistrates who should have been denouncing the whole affair.

The backers and their friends had arrived in the outer ring. Fifteen minutes to go before the twelve-stone Gasman, so named because of his flaring brilliance, did battle with the fourteen-stone, long-armed underdog, Bill Neat. The old boxers patrolled restlessly, fisting their way back through the years to their own entrances into the inner ring. And their exits.

"Five years' time and Hickman and Neat will be joining them," Blackstone said.

"Hickman maybe," Foley said. "He's too cocky by far. He's got some flash company, too. John Thurtell among them. Do you know Thurtell, Blackie?"

Blackstone nodded. "Went backrupt in Norwich and cheated his creditors. Moved to London and defrauded an insurance company of £20,000 by burning down his premises. A man born for the gallows."

"Well, he's helping to train Hickman."

"Then Hickman will have to keep a tight hand on his purse."

"If he wins."

"I thought you said he was a certainty."

"So he is," Foley said, trying to press a dent out of his hat. And then, seeking escape from the uncertainty that he had voiced, "Did you go to the coronation, Blackie?"

"Yes," said Blackstone. "Why?"

"I thought you might have seen the old fighters there guarding Prinny from the mob. Eighteen of them dressed as pages at the approaches to Westminster. It was grotesque, Blackie. Humiliating. But they must have been paid well." With thin fingers he massaged the small flushes seeking permanency high on his cheeks. "Very well paid, I should think. Josh Hudson, Tom Oliver, Bill Eales, Cribb, Tom Spring, Bill Richmond. . . ."

"A pity they didn't stay at home," Blackstone said. "Then we might have had another king."

Five more minutes.

Anticipation of blood and bravery was tight in the air. Crows hung lazily in the sky. A rumor that the Dragoons were on their way to stop the fight circulated and the magistrates retreated like tortoiseshells into their coats. A mudlark dredging in the trampled mud still concealing needles of ice, found a sovereign and departed. A pieman's oven caught fire. An organ-grinder's monkey escaped and danced from shoulder to shoulder chattering with fear of

13

his freedom. A novice trollop from Newbury offered to lift her skirts behind a hedge and was told to wait till after the fight. A thimble rigger caught rigging the thimbles escaped with a broken jaw. A small stand knocked together overnight fell to the ground slowly like an old man kneeling.

Four minutes to go; £200,000 said to have been staked on the fight.

Foley pointed to a disturbance among the gentry. A black figure was pushing its way between them, head down, swimming with his arms. Then he was through into the green moat of the outer ring.

Muscled guardians moved towards him. But Hansom held up his hand. He's mine, the hand said.

The Negro was about sixteen. He was bared to the waist, legs in faded breeches. He was lithely built but thin, the diet of the slums betraying his body. He brought warmth to the ring, the sunlight finding lights on his black skin, the frost on the grass becoming cotton in the field. His face was handsome and his teeth flashed brilliantly as he taunted Hansom.

"Good God!" Foley exclaimed. "Hansom will kill him."

Blackstone climbed out of the post-chaise, feeling in his coat pocket for his gilt-crowned baton.

Foley said, "You can't do anything, Blackie. You're not even supposed to be here."

"I'll have to."

"You'll have to stop the fight if you show yourself."

"Then I'll stop the fight."

"The Fancy will murder you."

Blackstone pushed his way through the rich and titled, hand tightly around the baton in his pocket.

The crowd was as silent as if the main fight was about

to begin. "Chuck him out, Handsome. But go easy, culley. He's only a lad."

Blackstone reached the outer ring. He saw the hatred in Hansom's face, knew that the old pugilist was looking into the victorious face of Molyneux, the American Negro.

The black stripling, watch-spring hair shining blue-black in the sun, shouted insults at Hansom; at his big belly, his slow fists. Hansom advanced, brushing with one hand at the dent on his cheekbone; hoping, probably, to grapple with the boy, to get him in a "suit of chancery," head under one arm, battering at his face with the other fist. Blackstone sensed more than a desire to punish: he sensed the greed to kill. He began to climb through the ropes when the Negro boy darted forward, hit Hansom on his expansive nose and danced away.

Hansom shook his head, puzzled. He tightened his fists and came on, a glowering old bull. The Negro sauntered within clouting distance, fists lowered. A Sunday-joint fist lunged but the black target had removed itself. A smaller black fist banged Hansom's ear.

The Fancy were beginning to enjoy it. "Come on, sambo. Give old Handsome a hammering like he handed out just now. Give him a mouse. But don't let him cuddle you or he'll kill you."

Hansom spat on his fists, looking much older now, belly forgotten again, breath like bellows, the yellow in his eyes noticeable against the quick whites and browns of his opponent.

The boy feinted with his left and let go his right, the knuckle sinking into the cushion of Hansom's belly. Blackstone retreated into the spectators. Reflexes, balance, speed, anticipation, mettle: they were all there. The style that was beginning to replace the rushing and hugging of

15

the traditional fighters; the style with which Neat hoped to overcome the Gasman's lightning grapples. Blackstone almost felt sorry for Hansom. But not quite.

The Negro was showing off now. Dancing around Hansom, stinging him with quick punches. Blackstone hoped that Hansom would catch him with one blow: it would do him good. The boy hit him in the belly again and the old fighter winced: that was the place to hurt him, not in the face, from which pain had been erased years before.

Hansom made one last effort, rushing at the Negro, heavy arms outstretched, hoping to catch him in a bear hug; to squeeze the green-stick ribs until they split. Instead he received a jab in the nose, which uncorked the blood, and another in the kidneys. As he lumbered by, the boy stuck out his foot and tripped him. Hansom fell heavily and lay like an upturned beetle.

An elegant man standing beside Blackstone struck his thigh with his cane and said, "A spirited lad. I'll wager there'll be a patron or two after him before the day's out."

"I shouldn't wonder," Blackstone replied. "Out for some sport before they cripple the lad in mind and body."

The Duke of Devonshire looked at him in surprise. "What the devil are you talking about? You're here enjoying the fight, dammit. If the boy's handled properly he'll make enough money in a short while to settle down and earn an honest living."

"If he's handled properly."

Hansom struggled to his feet. But the other fighters held the Negro's arms. Hansom took this as an invitation to hit him while he was pinioned. He moved forward, his punished face and body ugly beside the boy's ebony grace, blood bright on his white shirt. One of the younger guardians stepped between them shaking his head. The Negro was led away grinning. Or snarling.

16

The Duke clapped and the rest of the Fancy followed, the applause like a shower of rain getting under way. "The best beating out of the ring I've ever seen," the Duke announced.

His friends agreed. The Earl of Sefton, Lord Manners and the Duke of Beaufort.

Blackstone walked thoughtfully back to the post-chaise.

A man named Lawler was waiting for him. Gambler, part-time bookmaker, informant under duress. Not bad looking, it was doubtfully agreed, with dormant virility somewhere there; a man who left you with a feeling of unease, hands checking your pockets. When he acted a part—which he frequently did at Blackstone's insistence— he did it with accomplishment, a chameleon of human behavior. At the moment he was off-stage, colorless, absorbed with the profit and loss of small bets.

"Hallo, Mr. Blackstone," he said.

Blackstone nodded.

"You are sure, aren't you, Mr. Blackstone?" Once or twice he had called him Blackie, but this hadn't been encouraged.

"About what?"

"About the Gasman."

Blackstone tapped the door of the post-chaise. "We are sure, aren't we, Foley?"

Foley poked his mourning face out of the window. "Of course we're sure. Neat doesn't stand a chance. I shouldn't be surprised if Hickman doesn't floor him in the first round just like Jack Randall beat Jack Martin."

Lawler looked to Blackstone for further comfort. "But *you're* sure, aren't you, Mr. Blackstone? I've been a bit rash this time. You did promise me. . . ."

"Don't worry," Blackstone said. "Now I've got a little job for you, Lawler."

17

"What, now? Right before the fight?"

"Right now," Blackstone said. "Before the fight." He gave Lawler a sovereign, told him what to do and climbed back into the post-chaise, taking care not to soil his new dark blue, brass-buttoned swallow-tail coat made in Duke Street, or scuff his boots made by Hoby, the King's bootmaker, in St. James's Street.

"My!" Foley said. "You've become quite the Beau Brummel since you joined the Runners, haven't you."

"You can have the coat when it's thrown out," Blackstone said.

Neat arrived first, walking between his kneeman and his bottleman, threw his hat into the ring and began to undress. Then Hickman, sucking oranges and tossing the peel around, inspecting Neat as if he were a third footman on trial. They wore cotton drawers and woolen stockings; both well-sheathed with muscle, but Neat's torso, above the yellow Bristol colors at his waist, had a farmyard set to it compared with the Gasman's frame and flickering muscles.

The cornermen—kneeman to provide a knobbly stool for the fighter, bottleman to provide orange, sponge and bottle of whatever the fighter fancied—went to their corners.

They tossed for the sun—important on such a diamond-bright day—and Hickman won. Hickman the favorite, the indomitable, the Gas, lover of gin and success, the boxer who had already confronted his opponent in the Fives Court in Little St. Martin's Street, London, saying, "What are you, Bill Neat? I'll knock more blood out that great carcass of thine, this day fortnight, than you ever knocked out of a bullock's."

They went up to the scratch. They shook hands. They

began to fight. With the sun sliding away, leaving loneliness behind, the night's cold mustering its forces at 1 p.m., the crowd silent, including the monkey. Wagers irrevocably struck, feet ossifying in mud, even the premature trollop overawed.

Hickman flared first. He hit the farmyard Neat five times. Bone on bone. Neat fell, prising open the silence. The favorite couldn't lose. Optimists tried to lay money on Hickman; only fools offered odds.

A knock-down was the end of a round. Round one to Hickman. A thirty-second break with Neat on his second's knee and a bottle of unidentified liquid to his lips.

Foley said: "See?" He lit his pipe.

They were at each other again. Neat with his mutton fists at full length, his left a few inches above his right. Such long arms.

Hickman tried to get through the guard. They both landed, they both fell. Two rounds later Hickman threw a swift right to Neat's neck, but he couldn't force it through the Bristolian's reach; the return punch cracked Hickman on the eye. The gas flickered. Hickman fell to the grass, one side of his face blushing and swelling.

Another round. Hickman's right eye was closing, his cheek scarlet. He grinned grotesquely. The Fancy were in tumult, fortunes floating like the crows in the winter sky. The cold was crystallizing, but it was unnoticed.

Blackstone said, "What odds now?"

"You wait," Foley said, red patches on his cheekbones spreading under Neat's blows.

"I thought it was always six to four."

"Seven to four," Foley said. "If you want to have a bet on the side, that is."

"I don't," Blackstone said. He looked for Lawler, but

he had vanished, trying to assume the part of a man who hadn't laid a bet.

A couple of rounds later Hickman seemed to have rallied.

"Six to four," Foley offered, seeking more reassurance from his hip-flask.

Hickman pushed himself at Neat, seeking a throw or a "suit of chancery" or a lucky punch. But Neat stood back, dodged and felled the Gasman with his left. He had style, Blackstone thought.

There was a lot of blood around, as bright as holly-berries in the sun reaching for the horizon.

Foley said, "They can't take much more."

"Neat's got it," Blackstone said. He shivered with the cruelty and courage of it. Wondering at this lust; at such emotions which nudged the crimes of violence he was supposed to suppress. In any case he shouldn't be here, he remembered. It was his duty to implement the law regardless of his own views on morality; today he was aiding and abetting an offence. What authority would he have with criminals if they saw him condoning crime? But every crime has to be investigated. And that's what I'm doing, he lied to himself. That's what I'll tell them.

The twelfth round. The crows like vultures in the cooling sky. Sweat starting from the two fighters, their faces red and spongy, eyes slitted between mauve cushions. Their weariness reaching the crowds so that men grunted and cringed as the blows got home. It wasn't a particularly long fight, but few could remember such punishment given and taken.

The blow from Neat connnected with a thud on Hickman's face. Hickman stood swaying as if deciding which way to fall. Backwards it was. His eyes glazed, mouth seemingly filled with blood.

But the Gasman fought on and his cockiness was forgiven even by those who had backed him to win. Or most of them. At the eighteenth round the Gas finally failed.

Immediately they began to collect a purse for him and most of the true Fancy contributed. Blackstone threw in some coins; so did Foley, wiping the sweat which was in danger of frosting on his forehead.

"There goes your certainty," Blackstone said, pointing at the limp figure of Hickman being helped to a barouche.

"A brave fellow," Foley said, scraping at a bald patch on his coat with his thumb-nail.

Neat was covered in a greatcoat, drinking from a bottle, smiling with bloodied lips, grinning and waving at friends, resuscitated by victory.

Carrier pigeons loaded with the news of the fight rose into the sky, the crows wheeled away. The clouds on the horizon had frozen into alps. The crowds streamed away, exultant, despairing. The monkey shivered, and a queue of three who had backed Neat formed for the rustic trollop despite the stiffening breeze that smelled of night and cruelty. In Hungerford and Newbury and outlying villages the doors of the taverns opened like boilers opened for coal. Orange peel, tickets, song-sheets, sporting journals, chestnut skins, lay in the mud to be sifted by the mudlarks. Already they were dismantling the ring, destroying the evidence of this vast public misdemeanor.

Foley said, "Shall we be going?"

"In a minute."

"What are we waiting for?"

"Lawler," Blackstone said.

When nearly everyone had gone, and the alps had flushed a pink that did nothing to warm the evening, one figure remained. Lawler attempting the impossible role of winning gambler and failing this once.

21

"You promised me . . ."

"You're a gambling man, Lawler. You must know there's no such thing as a certainty."

"I took a lot of bets on Neat and put the money on Hickman."

"You're not the only one who lost."

"I thought you knew something."

"I thought I did. So did Foley here."

"But it's my living."

"More fool you." Blackstone leaned out of the post-chaise. "Did you get the information?"

"I got it all right. I think it's worth more than a sovereign. In view of the fact that you promised me . . ."

"The information, Lawler."

Lawler gave it to him. Blackstone gave him another ten shillings.

As the post-chaise bumped over the rutted turf Foley said, "I suppose a lot of people will regard Neat as champion now."

"I suppose so." Blackstone was writing down the information Lawler had given him.

"I reckon Tom Spring could beat him." Foley's sad features brightened infinitesimally. "I'll give you six to four."

2

Blackstone rode to the gymnasium near Barnet one March morning when snow was beginning to peel from the sky and settle hesitantly on the countryside.

His horse, the Poacher, galloped well, hoofbeats becoming muffled as the snow thickened, breath steaming thickly on the flaking air.

He passed some mouchers, hanging out their hats for coins and catching snowflakes; a band of Irish immigrants striking out from London to exchange city starvation for rural poverty; a column of bright gypsy caravans, the girls inside bright and gawdy this blind day.

The gymnasium, owned by a patron of pugilism, Sir Humphrey Cadogan, had been built well outside London to discourage the fighters in training from visiting the fleshpots—gin and women having lost many a fight, and a patron's money.

Sir Humphrey Cadogan was one of the six leading patrons in England, their numbers having diminished since the formation of the Pugilistic Club. He was in his fifties, florid, almost distinguished; aware that he was a shadow of the patrons of old renowned for their eccentricities. Men such as "Hellgate" Barrymore, the 7th Earl Barrymore, who supported a fighter called Hooper, the "Tinman," married the daughter of a sedan-chairman and accidentally killed himself in a carriage at the top of Folkestone Hill when a fusil he was carrying went off and shot him through the head. Patrons like Lord Hanger who married a gypsy, served in America with the Hessian Jager Corps, became equerry to the Prince of Wales, was jailed for ten months for debt, became a coal merchant shortly before succeeding to the title of Lord Coleraine. Patrons such as Robert Barclay Allardice, mentor of Tom Cribb and John Gully, who could pick up an eighteen-stone man from floor to table with one hand and once walked a thousand miles in a thousand hours.

Sir Humphrey Cadogan made up for his uneccentric personality with a zeal for reform, notably with fallen women. He was generous to his servants, a quirk often equated with eccentricity.

He had a daughter named Laura, and the memory of her made Blackstone urge on the Poacher through the snow.

An enigmatic girl, Laura Cadogan. Full of appetites, with hair that was coarse and shiny, a complexion as healthy as a dairy and breasts that pushed urgently at the silk of her dresses. But the collars of Laura Cadogan's expensive gowns made of Levantine silk or muslin were always high at the throat, as if she were ashamed of her body, her appetites and her sex.

At one corner of her mouth was a scar the size of a small coin. It moved when she spoke, laughed when she smiled, which was not often. She was the only child of Sir Humphrey, who was a widower, and Blackstone believed that her inhibitions stemmed from her father's zealousness.

24

A succession of fallen women—Blackstone suspected that most of them remained supine at Cadogan's mansion—could not have given her a balanced view of love. In particular she disliked the rakish masculinity of the Fancy.

Blackstone wanted to kiss the scar, then her lips. But too many men would have tried to kiss the scar first. Better to take the scar second.

Laura Cadogan was one good reason for riding through the snow to Barnet. Another was an urgent summons from Sir Humphrey Cadogan. The third was the fact that Blackstone's protégé, the Negro boy who had fought Hansom at Hungerford, was training at the gymnasium.

She was waiting for him in the flag-stoned hall of the mansion—a contented, red-bricked place veined with ivy, its windows sleepy and lidded with blue shutters. Its comforts were emphasized by the snow creeping up the window-panes and sealing an envelope over the roof.

She was dressed in fashionable "celestial blue," tight around the bust, prim around the neck, a beautiful gown with flounces and leg o' mutton sleeves.

She waited while a pale dollymop who knew her place took Blackstone's snow-plastered riding-coat and hat which looked like an iced cake. Before she left their presence, almost obeisant—because Cadogan paid her the handsome salary of £10 a year—Blackstone retrieved a Manton pocket pistol from his coat.

"Are you going to shoot someone?" Laura Cadogan asked. She stood in front of the fire, warming her hands. She poked the logs and spirals of sparks whisked up the broad chimney.

Blackstone grinned. "I don't like to be without a gun, however exalted the company."

"A barker, I believe it's called in the underworld." The button of a scar extended into a question mark. "Isn't that right, Mr. Blackstone?"

"You sound very knowledgeable about such matters, Miss Cadogan."

"I've been studying the criminal classes, Mr. Blackstone. But my knowledge must be poor compared with yours."

Blackstone agreed that it was. He suggested that he might be able to teach her more.

"Perhaps." The voice of a woman recognizing a ploy. "I've been reading a book about cant."

"Ah."

"The salt-box, Mr. Blackstone?"

"The condemned cell."

She looked disappointed. "A glim?"

"A light. It's also a way of begging by pretending you've been left destitute by a fire. And it's also . . ." He decided against the third meaning.

"Is it something I shouldn't know?"

Blackstone said it was.

"Something a *woman* shouldn't know?"

He nodded.

"Come, Mr. Blackstone, I know a good deal. I am, after all, the only daughter of a reformer." The scar gave her voice a slight slur which was not unattractive. "I see and hear a lot of unsavory matters that a *woman* shouldn't hear."

Deftly, Blackstone took over the questioning. "A fine wirer?" he asked.

"An accomplished pickpocket." The diction, despite its slur, backed by a childhood of nannies and tutors. She thought for a moment and added, "In particular a pickpocket who steals from women." Not necessarily worse

26

than stealing from a man, she managed to imply. "The shinscraper, Mr. Blackstone?"

"The treadmill." He decided not to tell her that it was also known as the cockchafer.

"You must send a lot of people to the treadmill."

"A few."

"And are you proud of it?"

The game, Blackstone decided, was over. "Is your father available?"

"He said he would send a maid along when he was ready to see you. But you didn't answer my question. Are you proud that you have the power to send men and women to the treadmill? And the hulks and the gallows," she added.

Blackstone took some snuff from his gold Nathaniel Mills box. "Look," he said, "the treadmill disgusts me. I'm not a great lover of the hulks. Or a house of correction, for that matter. They should be reformed, I'll grant you. But first, for God's sake, guide this reforming zeal which you share with your father in more worthy directions. Have you, Miss Cadogan, ever been in a Rookery?"

She said she had and this surprised Blackstone.

"And you weren't accosted, robbed, spat on?"

"None of those things, Mr. Blackstone."

"Then you haven't been in a Rookery."

"I assure you I have." She sat on the leather seat on the brass bedstead of a fender. "I give you my word. Would you like some tea?" Very cool, all emotions suppressed.

"No tea." He fingered the warm gold of the snuff-box. "Very well, there should be prison reform. Criminal reform, too—and Peel will see to that. And your father doubtless does excellent work in the fancy houses." He looked to see if she recognized the phrase: he thought she

27

did. "But what about a little zeal directed towards the beggars in the Rookeries? The children sent out in Pentonville with charcoal under their eyes to make them look consumptive." He stared at the snow pouring from the sky. "They'll be out today, you know, Miss Cadogan. And a few will doubtless freeze to death. If they're lucky they'll make enough money—after their patron has been paid—to thaw out in a twopenny lodging house. Although they may well suffocate there or pick up some disease which will make the charcoal under their eyes unnecessary." His fists were bunched and he paused for a moment.

Infinitesimally, Laura Cadogan's face had softened. Or it may have been the firelight playing tricks.

"And animals," Blackstone said. "Perhaps some reformation could be extended to them. They haven't committed any offences, unlike those treading the mills. Have you ever been to a slaughter house, Miss Cadogan?"

She shook her head.

"Did you know that in one underground slaughter house close to St. Paul's they throw the sheep in so that they break their legs first. Then they knife them and flay them. Incidentally," he added, "the current payment for killing and dressing one sheep is 4d." Deciding that he was becoming too explicit he said, "I'm only telling you these things because you say you've been to the slums. You were very lucky to get out again, Miss Cadogan."

"I suppose I was." She was subdued. "You're not quite as I imagined the first time we met, Mr. Blackstone."

"Who is?" He sat opposite her on the other arm of the fender. "All I'm trying to say is that we should first show compassion for the victims of our society rather than those who capitalize on it." He thought he sounded pompous, the penalty of a mongrel education: trying to ascend the towers of Oxford from the gutters of Holborn.

A bell rang deep in the quarters of the well-paid servants and a maid with bonnet askew darted into the hallway peopled with portraits of zealous Cadogan ancestry. She curtsied and announced that the master would receive Mr. Edmund Blackstone.

Laura Cadogan stood up. Face flushed from the fire, contempt still signed by the scar. But subdued. "It's been an interesting chat, Mr. Blackstone."

"Perhaps we could talk again?" He wanted to kiss the scar. "It's unusual to find someone like yourself interested in the *deprived* classes."

"We're an unusual family, Mr. Blackstone." She paused. "I suppose you're a devotee of sport. Prizefighting. A member of the Fancy?"

Canny Bow Street instincts were alerted. "Not prizefighting, Miss Cadogan. A brutal and sadistic sport."

Which it was.

Sir Humphrey Cadogan looked fit for his age, except that his color was too bright above the white collar sawing at his ears. The fitness came from horse-riding and fresh air breathed at prizefights up and down the country: the color came from his liking for bloody beef and claret. He was still handsome, with a noble nose and grey hair combed forward; but there were signs of the zealot in his features—the call that comes to some men to reform the world while selflessly excluding themselves from the reformation.

He had agreed to masquerade as patron of the Negro boy whom Blackstone had seen at the Hickman–Neat fight fifteen months earlier, and arranged to meet through Lawler. If he didn't, he had inferred from Blackstone, there was a strong possibility that the Dragoons would break up any fights where his pugilists were fighting.

Blackstone, who was financing the Negro, needed anonymity—a Bow Street Runner couldn't encourage an illegal sport—and Cadogan's training facilities. Although he wasn't happy about the training.

But the summons from Cadogan to Blackstone's rooms in Paddington Village had nothing to do with prizefighting.

Cadogan was sitting in front of a coal fire in his study smoking a clay pipe and drinking brandy and hot water spiced with cinnamon. His face was more flushed than usual and there was a smell of cheap scent in the air as if Cadogan had been in intimate conversation with one of the girls he saved in the Haymarket, the Strand, Covent Garden or even Seven Dials.

Blackstone sniffed the air as he entered the room.

Cadogan stood up, adopting a buttock-warming pose in front of the fire. He noticed Blackstone sniffing and remarked: "She's a poor girl. I found her in Kate Hendricks' place behind Leicester Fields. Do you know it, Blackie?"

Blackie did know it, and doubted that the girl was poor in any sense that required compassion. Many of the whores walking the streets—particularly the children—did deserve pity. But not the ladies employed by Mrs. Hendricks.

Mrs. Hendricks, a rouged jelly of a woman, presided on a platform drinking champagne through the night with her friends. They looked down upon a gaslit concourse of bare-shouldered bawds with emerging busts platformed on whalebones, and raffish men, some with opera hats and white waistcoats. The air was clouded with tobacco smoke and a bottle of champagne cost twelve shillings. Mrs. Hendricks made most of her money from the champagne, bad as it was expensive, and the whores made it as quickly as their prowess enabled them.

No, Blackstone thought, he hadn't come across many "poor" girls at Kate's.

"What are you going to do with her?" he asked.

"First show her some kindness. Then put her in touch with one of the societies that will find her a post in service. I only wish I could keep all these poor girls in my own employ."

Blackstone didn't doubt it. "I can never understand," he said, "why you're so concerned about some vices and yet you encourage prizefighting."

"Nothing wrong with pugilism." Cadogan lifted the tails of his coat the better to toast himself. "It's manly, it's fair, it's a test of skill and endurance. In other words, it's sporting." He pointed at the prints on the walls, among them a picture of George IV, then Prince of Wales, entertaining the King of Prussia, the Czar of Russia and General Blucher with an exhibition of pugilism by Gentleman John Jackson and others. "It's only some out-of-date puritanical law that makes it illegal."

"I'm not sure it's as simple as that. There's too much crime every time there's a fight. And there have been too many deaths in the ring. I can't say that I'm proud of liking a spot of milling," he added.

Cadogan turned the subject a few degrees. "I gather you want to look after this sambo of yours yourself?" He poured them both brandy topped up with hot water, then sprinkled each with a pinch of cinnamon. "Isn't Donnelly"—his own manager—"good enough for you?"

"No," Blackstone said.

"What's wrong with him? At the Daffy Club—the Pugilistic Club even—he's considered to be one of the best in the country."

"If you think teaching a boy of eighteen to stand up

31

brawling and cross-buttocking without learning to use his legs, if you think stuffing him full of red meat and claret, with respect . . ."—he grinned—". . . is the essence of training then Donnelly's your man. Personally, I think the time has come to teach young fighters style. Balance, anticipation, footwork. The black boy's got talent but he isn't over-endowed with stamina. The result of being the son of a St. Giles blackbird and growing up on a diet of bread and watered ale and stew made from a dead cat after the pelt's been sold in Whitechapel. He's not built to brawl for thirty or forty rounds."

"Donnelly recommends red meat and claret to build up the young 'uns."

"I don't," Blackstone snapped. "And I want to take over the managing. I want that boy to have six good fights and make sufficient money to retire before he's twenty-five and put the money into a business. And I want him to retire before he's been beaten stupid. I want him to own a tavern like the Castle, not to beg in it like some of the wrecks from the ring."

Cadogan said, "Very commendable." But his thoughts had wandered elsewhere. He looked troubled. "Very well," he told Blackstone. "You can manage him if you like under my patronage." He walked to the window and gazed into the cold afternoon. After a while he said in a whisper, "On one condition."

Blackstone helped himself to more brandy. With the cinnamon it recalled Christmas: the Brown Bear Inn in Bow Street, the festive company of Ruthven and the other Runners, the loyal and ardent comforts of the girl who worked there.

He asked, "What's the condition, Sir Humphrey?"

Cadogan gazed silently at the courtyard where cherry-nosed servants' children threw snowballs and sucked their aching fists. Smoke from the batteries of chimneys on the roof swept down in a gust of wind and the snow changed direction. All that was missing was a robin.

Cadogan put his fingers on the window-panes as if testing their temperature. He said, "It's difficult . . ."

Which usually meant that a rich man who had been robbed wanted to do a deal if a Runner could act as intermediary, finding the thief and persuading him to return eighty per cent of the loot. The Runner took fifteen per cent, the thief was given five per cent and his freedom. A Parliamentary committee had taken note of this alleged malpractice among the Runners.

Blackstone told him, "I'm the soul of discretion."

He was surprised by Cadogan's reaction. He turned swiftly. "Are you, Blackie?" he asked. "Are you really?"

Blackstone hadn't meant it too literally. "I *am* a Bow Street Runner," he said.

This didn't seem to comfort Cadogan.

Blackstone spoke reassuringly, thinking of the Negro boy, Ebenezer Kentucky, sparring in the gymnasium across the courtyard. "What is it, Sir Humphrey? You can trust me—as long as you're not asking me to conceal a criminal offence. A grave criminal offence, that is." He guessed it was connected with a fallen woman; one, perhaps, who had picked herself up and objected to Cadogan's methods of salvation. "You're not being blackmailed, are you?"

Cadogan returned to the balm of the fire. "As a matter of fact," he said, "I am."

Cadogan offered Blackstone a room for the night, or for as long as he wanted to stay.

Blackstone looked at the countryside, settling for the

night with shadows in its white folds, and debated the invitation.

He thought about Laura Cadogan and accepted.

As he walked to the door of the study, Cadogan's confessional, he thought he heard a shuffling in the passage outside. He pulled the door open quickly and saw what might have been the flick of a coat-tail or a skirt vanishing round the corner of the passage. But he couldn't be sure.

He made for the gymnasium.

3

A couple of fighters, past their prime and bound for twilight rings, were sparring lethargically in one corner. One had a broken fist, barely mended, and he winced when his glove connected, which wasn't often.

Blackstone watched them with pity. Old-school fighters still brawling like Scroggins, uninfluenced by any of the finesse shown at the Fives Court exhibitions in Little St. Martin's Street, or the swift punch-throwing skills of the old champion, Jem Belcher.

No, this was the old Broughton technique, as subtle as a convict breaking stones. Writing in his book, *A Treatise upon the science of Defence,* in 1747, Captain John Godrey described Broughton's style:

> ... Broughton steps bold and firmly in, bids a welcome to the coming blow, receives it with the guardian arm; then with a general summons of his swelling muscles and his firm body seconding his arm and supplying it with all his weight pours the pile-driving force upon his man.

That was the sort of fighting that prematurely killed such men as Dutch Sam, Jack Randall "the Nonpareil," and Josh Hudson "the John Bull Fighter."

Blackstone was determined that Ebenezer Kentucky, "Ebony Joe," would not die prematurely.

He would have liked to have Ebony trained at John Jackson's rooms in Bond Street. Jackson taught guile and had been the poet Byron's "corporeal pastor and master." He taught amateurs and gentlemen; he taught them contempt of danger, he taught them to calculate punching distances, to use their feet, to be agile, to bend their bodies, keep their knees elastic and their fists up. But it was too dangerous: Blackstone was known there—and Ebony Joe wasn't tactful.

So it had to be the manor at Barnet where Blackstone's patronage was known only to Ebony Joe, Cadogan and Donnelly.

Donnelly was catching Ebony's punches on his left arm and countering swiftly with his right. Their feet hardly moved, sweat was pouring down Kentucky's face and spangling his watch-spring hair. His chest heaved, his guard dropped lower.

Donnelly was shortish for a boxer, but broad, his neck set in thick pads of muscle. His belly had thickened and he advised pupils not to hit him too low. He had a jockey's hooped legs, although thicker, and a lot of reddish hair on his chest. He had once hit an opponent in the crotch, kneed him as he grunted forward and clouted him on the back of the neck. The other fighter had died two days later. Donnelly, known in those days as "the Hooligan," immediately retired from the ring; although there were those who claimed he had already accepted a job with Cadogan.

Donnelly was inclined towards stage Irish. In liquor he sang and dashed tears from his eyes; he was also quick to fight, and quick to forgive when mollified with a pint of porter. He ducked direct questions as he had once tried to duck punches.

He spotted Blackstone, caught Kentucky a friendly cuff on the cheek and put up his gloved fists. "Good day, Blackie," he said.

"A word in your ear," Blackstone said.

"To be sure, Blackie." He gestured to Kentucky. "Go and get changed, boyo." As Kentucky walked away he said with a grin, "He's what I'd call a browned-off Irishman." He waited in vain for Blackstone to laugh.

They went to the far corner, away from the bruisers. The gymnasium smelled of oil from the lamps and stale sweat. There were old bloodstains on the floorboards, a few prints of fencing on the walls and some of the new dumb-bells lying beside some rusty foils. The dumb-bells had an unused air about them; because Donnelly would rupture himself if he tried to lift them, Blackstone thought.

Donnelly said, "What can I do for you, Blackie? Your man is shaping up quite well. He's a bit short on wind, though. But it's nothing that a diet of good red meat, porter and claret won't put right. Sir Humphrey's a great believer in the diet, you know."

"I'm not," Blackstone said. "Not that sort of diet."

Donnelly stopped for a fraction of a second as if he'd taken a blow in the belly. Then ducked and recovered. "Does Sir Humphrey know your views on diets?"

"He also knows my views on training. I'm taking over Ebony Joe's management, Donnelly."

Donnelly took a thirty-second break between rounds to muster an attack. "What does Ebony think about it?"

"I haven't told him."

"He seems quite happy with my methods."

"I'm sure he does. Any eighteen-year-old would be quite happy to train your way. But he won't be so happy when he's gasping after the fifth round at Moulsey Hurst and doesn't get his guard up quick enough to stop a bare fist taking out his front teeth. The boy needs building up, Donnelly. With good food by all means. But not jugs of claret. Most of all he needs exercise. The way Barclay trained Cribb to fight Molyneux. Nine weeks in the Highlands walking twelve miles a day. Then twenty. Plus a quarter of a mile run every morning and evening." Blackstone paused. "Did you know that in 1813 Sir Harry Smith, commander of Wellington's Light Brigade at Vittoria, claimed that any soldier was 'in better wind than a trained pugilist? He wasn't far wrong, Donnelly. Not if they're all trained by the likes of you."

"Has Sir Humphrey agreed to this?"

"He has."

"Then there isn't much I can say." He smiled, showing broken teeth with sawed edges which gave his face a vulpine look. "Not *here* anyway." The emphasis histrionic.

"Where then?"

But it was a direct question—an unfair advantage. "Are you staying the night, Blackie?" Familiarity as false as a forged sovereign.

"I asked you where you would have plenty to say?"

"Don't take on so," Donnelly advised him.

Blackstone took out the baton bearing the gilt crown and jabbed it in the feather-pillow of a belly. It sank in about two inches. "Where?"

Donnelly gasped, hatred sandwiched among the jocular creases of his face. "I was only thinking they would be surprised to hear in Bow Street that you were managing a prizefighter." He ran his tongue along the sagged outlines of his front teeth. "I mean it *is* against the law."

Blackstone nodded, jabbing the baton hard into Donnelly's belly again, "Don't try it, Donnelly. Just don't try it." He took out the Manton pocket pistol and examined it. "It's still possible to bring a prosecution against a boxer for killing his opponent during a fight."

"Jaysus," Donnelly said, "that was three years ago."

"Feloniously killing and slaying would be the charge."

"Feck you," Donnelly said.

"I take over Kentucky as from now," Blackstone said.

"You're welcome," Donnelly replied, eyes shifting from pistol to baton and back again. "He's too soft anyway."

"We'll see," Blackstone said, returning baton and pistol to his pockets and shooting out his cuffs beyond the sleeves of his dark blue Duke Street jacket. "Perhaps you'd like to lay a wager on his first fight?"

Donnelly, who had taken leave of his Irish charm, said, "Not with you behind him I wouldn't. Not with a corrupt Bow Street Runner behind him."

Blackstone took a handful of belly. "A what?"

"A Bow Street Runner," Donnelly said.

"Five pounds from you that says Ebony Joe won't win his first fight." He twisted his handful of flesh.

"Done," Donnelly gasped.

"Good man," Blackstone said, releasing him. "Now I'll have a word with Ebony as his patron *and* manager. And if," he added, "Bow Street ever gets to know about my dual role then I'll know who told them, won't I, Donnelly? Feloniously killing and slaying. You could get the hulks for that, Donnelly. Or the gallows."

The second obstacle to overcome in the new training regimen was Ebony Joe. At first when Blackstone offered to finance him there had been gratitude and some awe; but neither commodities lasted long in the Holborn Rookery where Ebenezer Kentucky had been brought up with his father, one of the St. Giles blackbirds—the Negro beggars.

They lived in a dosshouse, in a large room where a single fire burned. Sharing the room was a shifting tenancy of beggars, thieves, magsmen and macers, touts, sharpers, prostitutes, servants discharged without references, sweepers, mouchers, pickpockets. Ebenezer considered himself lucky: he learned the tricks of survival from the strolling players who shared the room, and he never shared a garret with thirty other urchins, crying out in nightmares which were little worse than reality. Also he could make good use of the kitchen fire, toasting bread, toasting his body and his wet, begging clothes.

Blackstone visited the dosshouse once. The room was choked with smoke and you could see the sky through the chimney hole in the roof. There were no floorboards and a worn wodden seat skirted the wall. When he arrived men with stubbled chins and greasy hair were toasting herrings; some in smocks, some in velveteen, one in an old blue flannel sailor's shirt, one in indefinable clothes, stiff with grease, wearing women's shoes cut away at the toes.

Among the ruined old coffee shops and fermented flash taverns of the Rookery, Ebenezer Kentucky learned the tricks of existence. Picking pockets, "lurking" a hard-luck story, robbing drunks, joining the toshermen scavenging the sewers, passing forged coins cut from pewter mugs in the Clock House in Seven Dials. Even the flashest of coiners allowed Ebenezer to watch them at work: they seemed to trust him with his black skin which never got blacker in the Rookery dirt. For all these benefits of birthright, denied to the less fortunate, Ebenezer Kentucky was grateful. And on Christmas Day, when well-dressed men and women with pulpit faces dished out

40

spitting sausages and hard potatoes baked in their jackets, Ebenezer thanked a nebulous god whose skin was sometimes black, sometimes white, always well-washed.

When he was about twelve, and this god wasn't looking, he pinched another boy's potato. The boy was fourteen years old and beefy: Ebenezer's father was thin, with ribs you could play a tune on and hair like grey smoke. Ebenezer planned to give his father the potato; but the boy caught him. They fought in the big room, the denizens cheering and placing wagers, the visiting well-wishers smiling wanly, and departing as grease from the frying pans spat at them.

Most of the money, much of it forged, went on the older boy, so beefy, Ebenezer thought, that *he* must have pinched a few potatoes in his time. The boy, whose name was Click, waded straight in, red fists pumping. Ebenezer dodged them with ease because it seemed more natural than warding them off; less painful too.

Click turned, slipped on some sausage fat and fell. Ebenezer kicked him in the crotch. Click rose and charged, face livid with pain. Ebenezer side-stepped and got home a blow on the ear.

"Come on, snowball," someone shouted.

"Come on, little 'un."

"Come on, Blackie."

Although most of them stood to lose money, all the support was for Ebenezer. He became exultant in his arena, smelling victory. Click caught him on the windpipe with the blade of his hand, then booted him in the ribs as he fell.

The cheers faded. Ebenezer's breath whistled sharply and he rolled, caught a flaying boot and brought Click down with him.

41

When they were on their feet again Ebenezer pretended to strike with his left. Click dodged to his left and Ebenezer hit him, drawing blood from his nose. He tried a similar maneuver and it worked again. When Click came at him he dodged out of the way. He swayed and pelted Click's suet face with sharp blows.

Until Click gave up.

Ebenezer handed his father the cold potato.

And found fresh horizons beyond the Rookery.

He frequented taverns owned by old prizefighters, picking up hints from them. He offered to fight young men brawnier than himself and received money from the Fancy for his courage. He ran errands, picked pockets and relieved drunks of their watches. He trained and took exercise, but not too much.

And all the time he made plans to become champion pugilist of the country.

But there were snags. Firstly, he wanted the glory too quickly; secondly, there was always a possibility that his training would be stopped if he was caught lifting watches; thirdly, he had sampled sex and liquor at an early age and was disinclined to sacrifice either.

Blackstone said, "I'm taking over, Ebony."

"I don't care who trains me," Ebenezer said, "as long as I get a fight soon."

"You're not ready yet."

"I gave those two a hammering." Ebony pointed through the doorway of the changing-room at the two sparring partners who had subsided on a bench.

"Don't feel proud of it." Blackstone sat opposite Ebony, who was buttoning up a pale blue shirt with a fluted front and billowing sleeves. *"They* were good once."

He sniffed the fighting odors of the changing-room which he had once briefly sampled. "Perhaps *they* started milling too young. Before they were properly trained."

Ebony buttoned his breeches, polishing the toe of each buckled shoe on his calves. His face was flat and handsome, but dodgy, always on the lookout—which was fine for boxing. The faces of white slum youths were sharpened by the necessity of improvising their poverty: Ebony's was flattened. But the effect—cocky and cunning—was the same. He was just eighteen.

Ebony said, "I must have a fight soon, Mr. Blackstone. A real fight." He traded a few punches with a phantom opponent.

"All in good time," Blackstone told him.

Ebony shook his head. "No, soon, Mr. Blackstone." He spoke with cockney accents, a slight molasses thickness to the vowels. "You see I need the blunt."

"I've given you money."

"I've spent it."

"What on?"

"This and that."

Blackstone shrugged. "Too bad, Ebony. But you needn't worry—you won't be spending anything on booze for a while. Or dollymops. You'll be laying off the girls for a while."

"I prefer to lay on them," Ebony said, catching his invisible adversary with a left.

"Have you read Mendoza's *Modern Art of Boxing?*"

"I can't read."

"Then we'll teach you," he said. Just like an old gentleman had taught him thirteen years ago.

"What does Mendoza say then?" Next to Molyneux and Richmond, Ebony admired Daniel Mendoza more than any other fighter. Blackstone wondered if he sensed discrimination against Jews, a feeling which wasn't extended to the blacks. Two years earlier Mendoza fought his last fight, aged fifty-five; a year later Gentleman John Jackson refused to let him use the Fives Court for his benefit exhibition.

Blackstone said, "He advised against excesses of food, wine and women."

Ebony said, "I'll go without the food." He flashed a smile.

"You'll go without all three. You'll exercise every day. A five-mile walk, a mile run. You'll eat a lot of steak, milk and fruit. And the occasional pot of ale," he added generously.

Ebony looked mutinous. He bunched his fists. "Strike me," he said, "that's too hard."

"Not for you, my culley."

"Who says so?"

"I say so."

"My patron? The arch-cove himself." Ebony paced the small room. "Supposing I was to peach on you, Mr. Blackstone?" He looked at Blackstone warily. "Supposing I was to tell certain gents that a Bow Street Runner was backing a prizefighter?"

Blackstone sat back and crossed his legs, smoothing the riding-breeches made by Beau Brummell's tailor, Mr. Weston of Old Bond Street. "Then you'd get your fight quicker than you expected, Ebony. With me. And after I'd flattened that nose of yours more than it's flattened now I'd arrest you for stealing."

"For stealing what?"

"One of my guns," Blackstone said. "I missed it from my rooms, Ebony. A 1785 flintlock converted to percussion by Perry. Single barrel, brass breech, patterned butt."

Ebony sulked. "I didn't think you'd miss it with all those barkers you've got."

"I did miss it. I thought perhaps you'd give it back. As you haven't I'll take it." He held out his hand. "Where is it?"

"In my room," Ebony said.

"Don't try and use it. You'll blow your brains out."

Ebony began to fill his stubby clay pipe. Blackstone wondered about smoking; but there didn't seem to be much harm in it.

Ebony said, "I still can't make out why you're doing this for me, Blackie."

"Mr. Blackstone. You're the last person who can call anyone Blackie."

"Why are you doing it, Mr. Blackstone?"

Because I was born in the Rookery, Blackstone thought. Or is it because I want to be patron and trainer of a champion? "Because," he said.

The snow had slackened and the bitter cold was free in the open spaces of the evening. The snow was a couple of inches deep—no longer wonderland stuff—covering the earth with a reminder of implacable rhythms: of a million winters to come, of the brevity of life and the eternity of death.

Turning up the collar of his riding-coat, Blackstone looked at the mansion, a refuge against assembling menace. A wind picked up a mare's tail of snow and spun it across the courtyard. By dawn many would be dead in the freezing gutters of the cities; and in country ditches they would also die, exhausted from a day smashing agricultural machinery depriving them of work.

In an upstairs window he saw Sir Humphrey Cadogan sitting at a table, a plateful of beef and a jug of claret doubtless in front of him. Blackmail didn't impair his appetites.

Blackstone walked across the courtyard, boots crunching on the snow, considering the threats. He wondered what to do if he caught the criminal and discovered how great were his needs compared with the victim's privileges. Was blackmail so much worse than lighting a fire under a chimney-sweep when he got stuck?

The cold is numbing my brain, he thought. He turned towards the lights of the village to find a tavern. The darkening fields stretched away to the knife-edge of the horizon. A cow lowed, a dog howled; but their calls were cut off by the night and buried in the snow.

4

The man with the long thumb-nail looked furtively at Blackstone. Blackstone knew the look: he carried with him the swagger of the law—and traces of a life the other side of it. Like the musk of the stables, Blackstone thought: lingering even when a groom is promoted to liveried footman. But the combination of underworld knowledge *and* authority gained him much respect. And much hatred.

Blackstone knew the man sitting across the tap-room was a thimble rigger; the man knew he knew. The pea—a pellet of bread, in fact—was concealed behind the long nail while a greenhorn tried to decide under which thimble it rested.

His face was vaguely familiar. A fairground face. It dodged, like a Christmas apparition, between drinking and dancing booths, peep shows, fire-eaters, sword-swallowers, strongmen, flea circuses. A standard face, sculptured with cunning and hunger, retaining the stroke of individuality with which each of us is signed and delivered. Wandsworth, Greenwich, Chapham, Mitcham . . . perhaps even Barnet Fair.

The thimble rigger grew more restless, made a pretense of looking for the serving girl and vanished into the night.

Blackstone ordered a Dog's Nose from the girl—flushed and flirtatious but lacking the inner gentleness of the girl from the Brown Bear—and spelled out the correct measures of warm porter, gin, sugar and nutmeg.

The tavern was like a stewpot in the middle of the countryside. Tobacco smoke, rum-sweet breath, gin fumes, farmyard clothes and steam from roasting meat the ingredients. In the inglenooks beside the log fire the old men who had roasted there for fifty years were almost done.

The girl brought Blackstone his drink. "You're not from these parts," she said.

Blackstone agreed he wasn't.

"I could see that a mile off. Those fine clothes. The way you speak." Some hair had escaped from her white cap, giving her an abandoned air. She lingered, ignoring other calls for service.

"That man," Blackstone said, "the one with the long thumb-nail who was sitting over there. Do you know him?"

The girl shook her head, disappointed at the turn of conversation. "Why?" she asked.

Blackstone shrugged. "It doesn't matter." He dismissed her but decided to bear her in mind if he were cut off by the snow.

He drank his sweet beverage and brooded upon the blackmailing threat to Sir Humphrey Cadogan, savior of fallen women (pretty ones preferably). As Blackstone had suspected, one of them had risen in wrath.

Cadogan had rescued Lily Spender from a Bond Street brothel flourishing behind the shop sign "First-rate milliner." He didn't explain what he was doing in a milliner's. He told Blackstone that he had brought her back to the mansion one summer evening, shortly after his wife's death, and had put her in the wing of the quarters of the well-paid servants where other ruined girls sojourned.

She was, said Sir Humphrey, sweet and spirited despite the degradation to which lecherous men and scheming madames had brought her.

The visit lasted a month—an average convalescence before Cadogan handed over a girl to other missionaries. He was, he explained, a middleman in good deeds. But he always took care to verify the credentials of the retailers before handing over his charges.

In the case of Lily—only seventeen although he had judged her to be at least twenty-two—he found a new channel for salvation. There was, it appeared, a great demand on the Continent for English actresses.

A theatrical agent named Meyning, of indefinite nationality, heard of Cadogan's crusading endeavors and suggested that he pass on any girls with acting potential.

Gratefully, Cadogan dispatched Lily. What followed was the version supplied by Lily to Cadogan.

First, she said, Meyning looked at her teeth to see if she was healthy. Then he asked if she really wanted to be an actress. She said she did and was taken home to meet Mrs. Meyning, who seemed a nice lady, but insisted on intimately examining Lily.

There was also the question of her age. Mrs. Meyning explained that on the Continent the employment of girls in their teens was frowned upon. But there were ways, Mrs. Meyning hinted. Had Lily got an elder sister?

Mrs. Meyning was delighted when Lily said she had. Together they went to Somerset House and obtained a copy of the sister's birth certificate. They were joined by Mr. Meyning and adjourned to a tavern where they drank "a lot of lush" and the Meynings asked Lily to call them uncle and auntie. Plans were made to catch the mail next day for the ferry to Boulogne.

It was only when she reached Boulogne, Lily claimed, that she realized she was being sold as a prostitute. "The very trade you were supposed to have rescued me from," she had shouted at Cadogan. And in reply to his protestations, "No, I didn't know actress meant bawd."

Meyning took her to Paris where she was examined by a French doctor, and rejected; although the rejection hadn't affected Meyning's sudden friendliness which developed whenever Mrs. Meyning was absent. "He's very fat and disgusting," Lily said.

The excursion culminated in financial disaster. Meyning tried to sell her at various Parisian bordellos, but she screamed about betrayal and the owners hastily withdrew. Finally he brought her back to London after she threatened to inform the gendarmerie if he deserted her.

On her return she heard about a commission investigating immoral traffic across the Channel and threatened Meyning with exposure. Apparently he paid up. Then, like any good businesswoman, she expanded her interests and threatened Cadogan.

Cadogan looked more saddened than outraged as he described Lily's behaviour:

"She behaved in a very common fashion, Blackie. A proper virago. She seemed to have forgotten everything I had done for her . . ."

Or done to her, Blackstone thought. "Did you know what Meyning's real trade was?"

Cadogan shook his flushed, aristocratic head. "Of course I didn't. Do you think I would have handed Lily over to him if I did? Dammit, Blackstone, I'm trying to

save these girls not return them to a life of debauchery."
He took a deep draught of claret.

Blackstone said, "In that case, Sir Humphrey, I don't
think you have much to worry about. It's your word
against hers."

"Not quite," Cadogan said. "Unfortunately Meyning
supports her story. I suppose they've come to some sort of
agreement. He says I knew that Lily was to be sold abroad
into the profession from which I'd saved her." Cadogan
stared into the rich depths of his drink. "And I've had a
threatening letter from Lily demanding money. It could
ruin me, Blackie."

"Hardly. A few lies from a trollop." Blackstone smiled.
"Albeit a reformed trollop. And some support from a cash
carrier—a man who lives off a woman's earnings," he
explained to Sir Humphrey. "Who would listen to that?"
Blackstone waited expectantly because he knew that there
must be more.

"Unfortunately," Cadogan said carefully, "I wrote a
letter . . ."

"Ah," Blackstone said.

Whatever your views on the victim, Blackstone thought
on his second Dog's Nose, it was still blackmail. A crime he
had been asked to solve on the reasonable understanding
that, as a Bow Street Runner, he would do his best. Also,
he conceded, bravery was involved whenever a blackmailed
victim approached the law. THE LAW. ME. Just the same,
who did you privately indict: victim or blackmailer? He
ordered another drink and watched the retreating figure of
the serving girl with an appreciation swollen by Dog's
Noses.

When she returned he asked, "How much gin are you
putting in these drinks?"

51

"It's not up to me," she said, one hip close to Blackstone's face so that he could feel its warmth.

"You have some influence, I feel."

She giggled. Blackstone didn't like women who giggled, but the girl's laughter wasn't unpleasant this wintry night.

"You could," she said, "put up here tonight."

A scar on another girl's mouth expressed contempt.

"Another time," he said, grinning as she flounced away.

He lingered, wondering about values. Wondering why a knight of Sir Humphrey's standing should have written a love letter to a whore.

He pushed himself out of the oven of the tavern into the becalmed night. The silence was thick, the snow creating its own light.

He turned up the lane towards the mansion, feeling his boots bite into the snow. Snow on the hedgerows moved and fell with velvet noise. An owl hooted.

A few flakes sidled from the watching night.

He stroke on with deliberation, feeling the glow of the drinks on his cheeks. He saw his own footsteps leading to the tavern blurred by the new flakes. He noticed other footsteps ahead leading back to the mansion.

Half an hour later he reached the servants' quarters where Sir Humphrey's women, exhausted by the ups and downs of their profession, were quartered.

Snow was pouring out of the sky now, and the lights from the windows, oil lamps and candles, burrowed into it.

He was hit first on the back of the neck, the blow cushioned by the upturned collar of his riding-coat.

As he fell he thought: I'm drunk. Instinctively his hand reached for the Manton pocket pistol. A boot swung in from the veil of snow, landing in his ribs. He waited for the boot to reappear, with one hand searching for the butt of the gun.

The boot lashed out again and Blackstone grabbed it with his free hand. His assailant swayed, fell with a thump, spraying snow about. He tried to pull his foot free but Blackstone hung on. Dimly he saw the extension of the man's hand: his gun—a holster pistol by the length of it.

Blackstone let go of the boot and swung at the wrist above the gun. He made contact, but feebly. The gun tilted forward as if the man's trigger finger had slipped.

The snow sluiced down from the close black sky.

Blackstone rolled to one side and fired through his coat. The night was illuminated, the snow scurring white insects; there was the mansion in all its contentment.

The ball smashed a window on the top floor.

A smell of scorched cloth. Burning on the hip. Red lights behind his eyelids. He became aware of his assailant groping in the snow for his gun. Doors opening, voices calling. And a masked figure fleeing into the night.

Later he thought about the gun that the man had dropped and asked a footman to retrieve it. He discovered that it was one of his own.

5

Laura Cadogan sat on the edge of the four-poster bed wearing more celestial blue. The room glowed with bluish snow light.

His neck was still sore but most of the pain had left with a sharp click that awoke him in the night. The main discomfort was the burn on his hip: he tried to persuade Laura to dress this without success. Cadogan's doctor offered to bleed him—he traveled with Cadogan and bled fighters when they were failing—but Blackstone sent him packing.

"Why should anyone want to attack you?" Laura asked.

"Perhaps he mistook me for someone else."

"It's hardly likely." She examined him dispassionately. "Six-foot-two with shoulders like a . . ."

"Prizefighter?"

The scar tightened. "I wouldn't compare you with anyone so depraved." Depraved, he noted, was a favorite word.

He said, "Why don't you tell me about it?"

"I suppose you want to know about the scar"—as if everyone did.

"About your childhood. If the scar forms part of it by all means tell me about it."

"There's not a lot to tell." Her tone contradicting her words. The lady's-maid hadn't dressed her hair and the ringlets were untidy, thick and blonde. Her face still bore the imprint of sleep.

"Then it shouldn't take too long," Blackstone said. He wore his jacket like a cape over one of Cadogan's nightshirts.

She shrugged. "Father used to take me along to the prizefights to meet all his cronies. He didn't see anything strange in it and it never occurred to him—or never seemed to occur to him—that it wasn't the life for a woman. I think he regarded me as his mascot. He didn't actually make me watch the fights, but the hotels where we stayed were full of the sort of people who enjoy that sort of depravity. The Fancy—you know what they're like."

Blackstone said he had an idea.

"As I got older a lot of the men, some of the fighters themselves, started to take an interest in me. I told father but he said that none of them dared molest me because they were too frightened of him."

"That doesn't sound like the attitude of the patron saint of fallen women."

"Yes," she said enigmatically, "I know about his reforms." She paused. "When I was fourteen one of his protégés got into my room in a hotel and tried to make love to me. I think he was quite a decent man really. But he had been drinking and I think some of the other men had put him up to it. For all I know I was the first girl he had tried to seduce. His name was Giles," she remembered. "Very strong, quite handsome in that sort of a way.

56

Anyway he started to maul me and I screamed. He put his hand over my mouth and pleaded with me to be quiet. I think, looking back on it, that we were as frightened as each other."

She was shivering, but not with the cold. He put out his hand to comfort her but she withdrew to the end of the bed.

Outside he could hear dripping: the thaw had begun.

"What happened then?" he asked gently.

"I kicked and struggled and got away from him. Although he must have let me because he was very robust. But I didn't realize that at the time. I was half crazed with fear. I grabbed the first thing within my reach, which happened to be a cup. It broke on the bedside table as I tried to hit him with it. He grabbed my arm and somehow I fell and the broken cup dug into the side of my lip. Quite deep," she said, trembling.

"I'm sorry," Blackstone said.

"You needn't be." Her face had lost its drowsiness and her body was taut. "It was a long time ago. I've got over it now."

Blackstone, who didn't think she had, said, "What did your father do?"

"That was the worst part of it. He went a little mad, I think. He got this boy Giles and put him in the ring with a big experienced bruiser and told them to fight it out. Giles didn't stand a chance. He was knocked down almost before the fight had begun. And then again and again . . ." She was beginning to cry. "He was beaten so badly that they said they thought his brain might be damaged. I don't think it was, though, because I saw him before he left. He managed to speak to me quite rationally and apologized

57

for what he had done. Or tried to do. . . . But his face was terrible to see. He had lost his front teeth, his eyes . . . well, you could hardly see his eyes."

"How do you know the details of the fight?" Blackstone asked, knowing before he had finished the question.

"My father made me watch. It was odd but he seemed to blame me as much as the boy. He even suggested that I had encouraged him."

"I see," Blackstone said.

He would have said more but a maid arrived bringing tea.

Later, when he was dressed—against everyone's advice—Blackstone told Laura he was returning to London. The snow was so soft now that it wouldn't endanger the Poacher.

Her reaction surprised Blackstone. "Then I'm coming with you," she said.

"Why, for God's sake?"

"I told you I had been to the slums but you didn't believe me. I also told you that I had been studying the cant of the poorer classes."

"Ah yes," Blackstone said, "the poorer classes."

She was sitting at a grand piano overlooking the melting garden. She had been playing, but not well, her fingers a little clumsy.

She said, "I have some work to do in London."

Blackstone made a guess. "Reforming?"

She nodded, a little put out, and played a few heavy chords.

"Everyone's at it," Blackstone said. "I suppose you inherit it from your father. What's it to be? The Society for the Abolition of the Treadmill? I can put you in touch with a gentleman who's already looking into the question at the House of Correction in Cold Bath Fields. Hippisley's his name. The men, it seems, experience great pain in the calves and ham . . ."

"And the women?" She looked hurt by his attitude. Blackstone was sorry, not sure about his motives.

"What sort of work were you contemplating?" he asked.

"There's a Society in Clerkenwell. They have all sorts of branches." She picked out a few crusading notes with her right hand. "One of the things we're trying to stop is prizefighting."

Sir Humphrey Cadogan was perturbed at Blackstone's impending departure. "The threats," he said, as they walked on the lawn, leaving green prints in the wet snow, "what are you going to do about them?"

"First of all I've got to find out who wrote the threatening letter. Obviously it wasn't the girl herself. I know of one or two screevers who would have done the job for her. They will know her whereabouts. It's a pity you didn't take some sort of action when she came to see you before she sent the letter."

Cadogan savaged a bush with his cane, causing a small avalanche. "What could I do?" His face looked very noble this morning, although the sunshine found the filigree of blood vessels on his neck and cheeks. "I couldn't hold her against her will." He turned and faced Blackstone. "All I want, Blackie, is that letter—the one *I* wrote. I know I was very foolish," he added, sensing Blackstone's contempt.

"Very foolish," Blackstone agreed, thinking that foolishness wasn't Cadogan's sole prerogative. He had left a pistol in the holster beside the Poacher's saddle for his assailant to help himself to. He said, "I'll have to have the threatening letter to identify the screever."

"When do you propose to go?"

"Tomorrow," Blackstone told him. "Early. First of all I've got some inquiries to make here. I want to find out who tried to kill me. And why."

A robin appeared in a bush beside them, happy with the thaw, showing that he was content to have them in his territory.

Blackstone said, "How many women have you got here at the moment? Fallen women, that is?"

"Two," Cadogan said. "Poor creatures, both of them. One from a house of ill repute in Windmill Street. And the other is from Kate Hendricks'. A poor creature who was well on her way to taking her profession to the Dials."

Blackstone nodded. He supposed that whatever happened to her in Cadogan's quarters was preferable to the Dials. "I want to see them," he said.

"Is it necessary?"

"Absolutely," Blackstone told him.

"Then I'll come along with you."

"I can't allow that," Blackstone told him.

The women were quartered between the footmen and the prizefighters.

The first was about seventeen, just managing to operate in Windmill Street, the haunt of child prostitutes. With the help of powder, poor lighting, customers' inebriation and an immature body she passed for fourteen—although this was a little old for Windmill Street. But she could no longer fake virginity, which was a pity because this was highly valued by gentlemen who believed it cured the clap.

Her name was Ethel. Blackstone estimated her professional expectation in the West End at about three years. From there she would drift to the docks, to the Dials, to superannuation, if she were lucky, keeping watch on street-walkers on behalf of a brothel owner.

She looked demure, a creditable feat for a whore quartered between footmen and fighters. She said that Sir Humphrey had been "very kind"—an attitude to which she was unaccustomed. She knew nothing of any threats to anyone and couldn't imagine who had attacked Blackstone. Threats, violence—it was beyond the comprehension of one so young and innocent.

The second woman was less demure. On seeing Blackstone she hurled herself at him, hands clawing, shouting, "Keep that bastard away from me."

Blackstone held her arms and pushed her gently but firmly on to the only chair in her small room dominated by a Crucifixion print above her bed and a bottle of porter on a table.

"I hear you're reformed, Amy," he said. And when she had quietened down he asked, "What story have you told Sir Humphrey, Amy?"

"The truth," she said. "Something that you wouldn't know about."

"The same story you told the magistrate, I presume?"

"The truth," she repeated.

Three years earlier, when he was on the foot patrol, Blackstone and the famous Runner Townshend had been assigned to delicate inquiries involving extortion from a Cabinet Minister. The Minister had met a girl at Kate Hendricks' and gone home with her. There, undressed and with a pistol stuck in the back of his neck, he had written a letter agreeing to pay the couple £500 and admitting intimacy with the girl, Amy Lawson.

The couple had been caught and, with the eminence of the victim in mind, an agreement had been reached. Amy and her conspirator had been sentenced to a year's imprisonment in a House of Correction on a minor charge of theft: the Minister's name had remained unsullied.

Blackstone, recalling Amy's plea to the magistrates, said: "A motherless girl from Wapping, wasn't it? Your father was a housepainter and one tragic day you met a woman who took you home to tea with her. There you were kept for several months until, your spirit crushed, you agreed to go on the streets." He watched her warily. "Is that the story you told Sir Humphrey, Amy?"

"I never went on the streets," she told him. "You know that. I went to Kate Hendricks'. I'm not just a common street-walker."

She hadn't looked too common when Blackstone knew her three years ago. Now she was a little over-ripe, ginny, on the route to the Dials.

"And to think I trusted you, Blackie," she said.

"It wasn't anything to do with me." The whole deal involving the Minister had disgusted him.

"You told me I'd only get a month."

"That's what I was told to tell you. That's what I thought you'd get."

She smoothed her plumage. "Anyway, what do you want with me now?"

Blackstone looked at her with qualified pity. "I want to know what you think you're doing here, Amy."

She turned professional, giving him a Kate Hendricks' wink.

"What do you think I'm doing, culley? I'm being saved." She poured herself a drink and offered the bottle to Blackstone; Blackstone refused. "Saved from a fate worse than death."

"A bit late, isn't it?" Blackstone said. He began to question her.

As he rode out of the gates a carriage followed. Inside it was Laura Cadogan. The driver carried a blunderbuss. Blackstone urged the Poacher towards London. There was drizzle in the air and slush underfoot. The Poacher's galloping hoofs made dirty splashes as the distance between carriage and horse lengthened.

In a snow-patched field Blackstone noticed a lone rider. Moucher, tinker, highwayman? Blackstone looked behind him. The carriage with its single driver-guard was about half a mile behind. With a sigh he reined in the Poacher and waited to act as escort.

6

A few days later Ebony Joe won a bout with Blackstone: he persuaded him to let him have a professional fight.

Blackstone agreed reluctantly and dispatched the chameleon Lawler, in the guise of Sir Humphrey Cadogan's agent and scout, to find a suitable opponent. Lawler was instructed to find a pugilist who would decently lose to Ebony without inflicting too much punishment. "I don't want the fight rigged," Blackstone warned Lawler. "I just want Ebony to win."

Lawler, already the agent of a famous patron, looked knowing.

"And I don't want my name connected with the fight in any way."

Lawler said, "I'm well aware of that, Mr. Blackstone." The role of the trusted, well-paid servant belied by the poor room in the Rookery, the thrush singing in its cage, bubble-and-squeak spitting in the crusty pan.

Blackstone considered those who knew about his prize-fighting activities: Cadogan, Ebony Joe, Donnelly, Lawler and Foley. They had one thing in common—none of them could be trusted.

"What about another sambo?" Lawler asked, flopping potato and cabbage on to a dirty plate.

Blackstone shook his head. "In the first place they'd hurt each other too much—heads like rocks. Secondly I want the fight to attract a certain amount of notice. So it's got to be black versus white. I want Ebony to establish himself on the first rung of the ladder to the top. But," he added, "I don't want there to be too many rungs."

"I understand perfectly," Lawler replied in his new voice. "An older fighter, perhaps?"

"No. They're too tough." He paced the small basement room pasted with sporting newspapers and prints. "No, it'll have to be someone about Ebony's age. A little older perhaps. Someone who's improving so that the fight has some meaning. For the championship of the future— something like that."

Lawler waited respectfully.

"A young fighter still using the old methods. That's it. The sort of fighter Donnelly would train. Give me six weeks or so and I'll have Ebony as agile as a mosquito round a bumble-bee. What's more we'll be helping to make boxing an art, not just a slogging match."

Lawler was temporarily overcome by the *we*.

As they left the room the thrush was still singing, as if the room were a spring garden dripping after a shower.

Lawler went straight to the Daffy Club in Tom Belcher's public house, the Castle, in Holborn, named after the Fancy's favorite beverage, daffy; also known as blue ruin, white tape, stark naked, flash of lightning, Fuller's earth, or just plain gin.

He took a seat at the long table known as the ring, ordered himself a glass of daffy, and waited his opportunity. But no one approached the titled patron's agent, seeing instead the familiar figure of a fringe bookmaker never too keen to pay out.

The Fancy had gathered in strength, mostly discussing the forthcoming fight between Bill Neat and Tom Spring. Coster-mongers, thieves, clerks, a muscly-necked navvy or two from the canals, a highwayman, market men, watermen, flue-fakers. Also a few swells in tall hats with aloof brims seduced from the Pugilistic Club by the cruder tastes of gambling, the stuff from the barrel instead of the bottle.

Lawler spotted Pierce Egan, the journalist, and Jemmy Soares, bum-bailiff and President of the Daffies.

And in a smoky corner, beneath a picture of Trusty, the dog who had won fifty sporting battles, Ebenezer Kentucky, soon to be launched as Ebony Joe, in deep conversation with a man whom he identified as Donnelly the manager.

Lawler wasn't sure whether they had noticed him; whether, in fact, Ebony Joe even knew him. But it was a meeting which had to be reported to Blackstone. He might even thank me, Lawler thought.

He ordered more gin and listened inattentively while a butcher who had lost all his meat and money gambling asked him if he thought cat-fighting was legal. He had, Lawler gathered, the biggest and most bellicose puss in London, matured on lites and liver, its fury sharpened by sudden famine.

Ebony Joe and Donnelly eased their way through the throng, pausing under a full-length portrait of Gentleman John Jackson (F. C. Turner after an oil painting by Ben Marshall). They shook hands, as if a deal had been concluded, staring into each other's eyes with a frankness indicating complete distrust. Or perhaps they were merely bidding farewell. They left without looking in his direction.

Above the murmur of talk—"I'll give you two to one, I'll give you six to four"—Lawler heard the insistent voice of the butcher. "Well, what do you think? You for instance—would you put a cat up against my Jem?"

"Not if he's as good as you say he is," Lawler said.

"He's a Bristol cat," the butcher said, sealing the puss's prowess.

Lawler took the point that the best prizefighters were Bristolians. "And the property of a butcher. Neat's a butcher, isn't he? And Spring. The battle of the butchers."

His companion nodded earnestly. "All the best fighters were butchers. Jem Belcher, Josh Hudson, Cy Davis, Jack Payne . . ."

"Not all of them," Lawler interrupted. "Don't forget the coal heavers and the navigators and the bargehands. Still," he conceded, noting the size of his companion's fist round his tankard, "a butcher from Bristol has to be reckoned with."

"I'm putting everything I've got on Neat," the butcher said. "Most of us meatmen are."

Lawler, who was backing Spring, said it seemed a good idea. He ordered more gin and bought Jem's owner a pot of ale. "Did you do any milling?"

"A bit. I could have become champion but I broke my hand on an Irishman's head. Still, my lad's a future champion if ever there was one. He's already making a name for himself."

Instincts which kept Lawler on the border of self-preservation—but not much further—stirred. "What weight is he?"

"On the light side," the butcher said. "Surprising really, a butcher's son. Takes after his mother, I suppose."

"Is he one of these new stylists as they call them?"

"Not on your life." The butcher was contemptuous. "He's being brought up the good old way. Clout your man as hard as you can, get him on the floor as soon as possible."

"If he's doing so well why are you broke?"

The butcher, whose name was Houseman, stared into his empty tankard. "I didn't realize how good he was and I didn't back him. But he's won two fights and a lot of folk think he's a future champion."

"Have you got him fixed up with another fight?"

"Not yet. I'm looking for a backer. A rich one. Although I'll look after the training."

"Mr. Houseman," Lawler said, standing up, "I think I may be able to help you."

"You mean you think cat-fighting's legal?"

Promotion for the Houseman–Kentucky fight proceeded with the usual odd mixture of caution, because of the law, and ballyhoo.

Blackstone told Cadogan to keep his side-stake down to £10 to deflate Ebony's self-importance. The other £10 was put up by Sir Nathaniel Tuxtall, Old Etonian, scholar, Member of Parliament, balloonist and dedicated eccentric.

Above all Tuxtall loved a sport in which sportsmanship was second only to brutality, and he gave articulate support to William Wyndham—ingenious, chivalrous, and high-souled, according to Macaulay—when he successfully opposed the bill in the Commons to abolish bear-baiting.

The articles were drawn up in the Daffy Club and the money was lodged with the landlord, Tom Belcher, brother of the late champion Jem. The date was fixed for late April, before the Fancy became too absorbed with the Neat-Spring contest. The venue was set "within 100 miles of London" to forestall any attempts to stop the fight by any vigilantes who might have got wind of it, a likely eventuality as details of the match were published in the sporting Press including the new *Bell's Life in London*. The two patrons, both eminent in the Pugilistic Club, wanted the fight to be held at Moulsey Hurst near Bushey Park because the site was under the patronage of the Duke of Clarence. This gave it a certain immunity against the law (in one year there were twelve uninterrupted fights at Moulsey), an immunity aided by a ferry which broke down if magistrates wanted to cross.

But again Blackstone objected to protect Ebony's ego. So the "100 miles" was narrowed down to Epsom Downs. And the contest between Ebony Joe, the Black Terror of St. Giles, and Bloody Billy, the Bristol Butcher, was relegated to a bout supporting the principal fight.

But within days of Ebony's match being struck the fight caught the imagination of the Fancy and there were reports of large sums of money being wagered. It puzzled Blackstone. He asked Foley, the professional gambler, and Lawler to find out why a supporting fight had attracted so much attention. They both returned with the same explanation: a mysterious gambler had laid out £5,000.

"But why this fight?" Blackstone asked.

Foley and Lawler shook their heads.

"Who's he backed to win?"

"Houseman," they told him.

"And you've no idea who he is?"

They shook their heads.

Blackstone took Lawler's arm. "Then find out," he said.

7

In his rooms in Paddington Village, Blackstone replaced the pistol "borrowed" by Ebony Joe and examined his collection of guns with pride. He was glad he lived in an age of change and acknowledged his debt to the Reverend Alexander Forsyth who introduced the percussion lock. He possessed several conversions; for the day ahead he chose two pocket pistols, one by Barber of Newark and, inevitably, one by Manton. He also took out the eighteen-inch French naval dirk, its blade patterned in blue and gold at the base, which he carried inside the soft leather of his boots.

He selected his clothes with care—wine-colored swallow -tail coat, white cravat—and remembered the days when he had dressed in moulting black velveteen and patched breeches with a stolen handkerchief at his throat.

As he dressed he assessed the day's priorities. A training session with Ebony, a visit to Laura Cadogan at the headquarters of the reformation society in Clerkenwell, a call on the screever whom he suspected of writing the threatening letter to Cadogan, a summons from the magistrate in charge of the Runners, Sir Richard Birnie.

71

Too many engagements: one would have to be dispensed with. His immediate reaction was Birnie. But there was his baton lying beside his guns: Birnie's summons would have to be answered.

The girl in the bed stirred drowsily, one sleepy breast above the coverlet. She gave a satisfied smile as she remembered the events of the night and beckoned Blackstone. He shook his head, still working on a compromise for the day. You had to be practical. The girl in the bed, who worked in the Brown Bear, hadn't really prepared him physically for a training session; or, for that matter, for a visit to Laura Cadogan.

He worked it out rather cleverly, he thought. He summoned Ebony Joe from the spare room, where he was now quartered, and told him to make his training run this morning to Clerkenwell and deliver a message to Miss Laura Cadogan regretting that urgent business with a screever in Soho made it necessary to postpone his visit.

Ebony Joe meaningfully glancing at the girl who had popped her breast back inside the bedclothes. "I wanted to have a word with you, Mr. Blackstone. About this training. I don't think it's doing me any good." Sharp Cockney vowels occasionally surfacing above the molasses. "They say the Butcher's putting on weight."

Blackstone held up his hand. "Not now."

"But, Mr. Blackstone . . ."

Blackstone, sensing trouble ahead, repeated; "Not now, Ebony." To mollify him he added, "I'm sure Houseman's putting on weight in the wrong places. In the belly probably so that you can sink your fist into it."

Ebony Joe remained unsmiling, muscles taut under his cotton vest. He turned on his heel and went out banging the door.

72

Blackstone went to the window and watched him jogging down the street, ignoring the urchins pointing at him.

The girl said, "Are you coming back to bed, Blackie my love?"

Blackstone said he wasn't, although she looked milky-warm and comfortable this brisk March morning with a high wind brooming away the night. He shaved and made some tea in the kitchen.

When he returned the coverlet had fallen away from both breasts.

"It's good, isn't it, Blackie?" she said. "You and me together like this." She beckoned a future of love and kindness and security. With little hope.

Blackstone handed her a cup of tea, fondling her breasts while she drank it. "Yes," he said, "it's good." Without projecting the goodness any further.

She put down her cup and asked, "Who's this Laura Cadogan?"

"A woman," he told her. "A reforming spirit hellbent on flattening prizefighting. She also wants to put an end to bull- and bear-baiting, dog-fighting, ratting and gambling in general. Although she doesn't seem so concerned with children forced to beg half-naked so that they shiver nicely, or baby farmers who leave the babies to die in cardboard boxes."

"You don't like her very much?" the girl asked hopefully.

"I don't admire her."

"Is she attractive, Blackie?"

If you lied it was a sort of defeat. "Very," he said.

She removed his hands from her breasts.

"Do you still want me back in bed?" he asked.

73

She turned her back on him.

He sat thoughtfully for a moment. The training session and the visit to Laura Cadogan had been dispensed with. He didn't have to see the screever in Soho until the afternoon, he didn't have to see Birnie until the evening. He had time on his hands.

He took off his clothes and got back into bed. After a moment or two she turned round to him.

Blackstone took a hackney carriage to Soho, sitting back, hands on the cane between his knees, breathing deeply of the spring air. In the park the dandies and ladies on horseback were appraising each other while, on foot, soldiers in scarlet hunted nursemaids and dollymops. The wind lifted the skirts of the last snowdrops, splayed the crocus petals, and sent clouds bowling across the blue sky.

His destination: a public house in Soho where a Mr. Shoemark carried on two professions. He was first and foremost a screever, penning begging letters, testimonials and other documents for the illiterate. He charged ninepence for a letter of average length and could supply a genuine signature from a defrocked clergyman or disgraced attorney for an extra shilling, or a forged signature of a celebrity for half a crown. For the Duke of Wellington's signature he charged three shillings.

His office was a table and chair beside the fire in the parlour where he worked until 2 p.m., one side of his face mottled by the heat. Then he went upstairs to his room, for which he was charged a nominal rent, where he bought and sold rats. He dealt in them in the hundreds, keeping his supplies in large mental-lined crates in a yard behind the inn, and a few specimens in his room. He preferred to deal in barn rats caught in the country: they were more profitable and hadn't the unmistakable odor of the sewer rats of London. He usually bought at 1s. 6d. a dozen and sold for half a crown.

Shoemark acknowledged his good fortune in being allowed the run of the pub; but he also knew his worth to the publican, an ex-prizefighter named Mellor, who ran the premises as a ratting house. There weren't many men who had such a way with rats as Aloysius Shoemark.

When Blackstone arrived the wind was tugging at a poster on the door. "Ratting this afternoon. Special attraction. Handsome prizes to be awarded for best dogs under 13½ pounds killing the most of these pestilent vermin." The master of ceremonies was to be Mr. Shoemark or, as he was known affectionately, "King Rat himself." A legend underneath in Mr. Shoemark's curly handwriting promised a plentiful supply of rats for gentlemen to "warm up their dogs with."

"Why in the afternoon?" Blackstone asked Mellor, who wasn't overjoyed to see him. "It's usually in the evening."

Mellor, a Welshman and a former lightweight, eyes hooded with scar-tissue, said, "It's an experiment. Two days of afternoon ratting that will probably continue into the evening. There's so many out of work these days that they have time on their hands." The song of the Welsh voice was sly in his possession.

"Where's the screever?"

"Mr. Shoemark's out at the moment. Buying a cartload of rats I believe. We'll need plentiful supplies, you see." He poured Blackstone a hot gin and water. "Will you be staying to watch the sport?"

"Perhaps." Blackstone enjoyed ratting as much as bull- or bear- or badger-baiting, which was not at all.

"You're not here on official business, are you?" He refilled Blackstone's glass and Blackstone didn't bother to pay.

"I could be," Blackstone said.

"Rats are vermin, Blackie. You know that. They've got to be killed somehow. Why not give the people some harmless fun at the same time? God knows, man, there's not a lot of it about these days."

"When will the screever be back?"

"Just before the dogs go to scale. About 2.30 I should say."

Blackstone looked at his watch. It was 2 p.m. "You won't mind if I go upstairs?"

"What for?" Mellor polished tankards, scrutinizing Blackstone from beneath tender hooded skin.

"Because," Blackstone said, "I have a mind to. And if you try to stop me I'll put a stop to your ratting festival and start inquiries to see if you're suitable to hold a license."

The Welshman examined a deformed fist. "Do whatever you please. You Runners always do, don't you?" The lilt in his voice discordant with hatred. "But there'll come a day mark you. I hear there's a few inquiries under way already."

"You hear too much for your own gool, Mellor." Blackstone finished his gin. "Which room does King Rat curl up in?"

"Number thirteen," Mellor said. "But I'm not giving you permission, mind." The lilt came down a key. "Illegal entry. It's against the law, isn't it?"

"Against the law, Mellor? Against the law?" He laughed. "What would you know about that?" He paused.

76

"Now you stay here, Mellor, polishing your tankards. Don't follow me up and don't let anyone else follow me up."

Mellor raised one hand loaded with a pewter tankard as if to strike Blackstone, then went on polishing. The tankard was beginning to look very clean.

Blackstone climbed the winding stairs cautiously. Although it was only 2 p.m. there was a dead feeling about the upstairs rooms. No servants, no noise; corpses lying in the bedrooms, verminous eyes watching from the shadows. It was dark, too, in the windowless corridor above the rat pit; the air smelled of freshly mixed whitewash.

Ten, eleven, twelve . . . Blackstone pushed the door of No. 13. It gave a little, but it was locked. He took out his twirls, the keys which opened most simple locks. The lock clicked and he stepped into King Rat's den.

A large brown rat dropped from the table where it had been nibbling a candle and darted into a cupboard where it disappeared through a hole in the floorboard. Blackstone pictured Shohmark tickling the rat behind the ears and teaching it tricks.

In the corner stood a narrow bed covered with a straw mattress and a coarse blanket. A gutted candle stood in a saucer on a chair beside it.

Light from a skylight fell on the table littered with papers. There was a battery of pens and a pharmacy of inks, red, green, purple. Also some worn seals, wax and a roll of pink tape.

Blackstone had stood uninvited in many unoccupied rooms. Standing alone in the undisturbed air he felt for the motives of the occupant; his ambitions, his regrets, his soul. . . . Here he experienced no such desire. To have done with the quest, to be out of the room—these were his dearest wishes.

He began to sift through the papers with reluctant fingers, looking for the list of names and addresses of clients that a man like Shoemark would keep. Because the Shohmarks of this world made a speciality of blackmailing those who enlisted their help to blackmail.

On top lay a sheet of paper on which Shohmark had been practicing signatures. Among them the signature of George IV. Either Shoemark was possessed of insane ambition or there was a gleam of humor in his rodent mind.

A cloud obscured the sun and the light from the skylight dimmed. Blackstone lit the candle. Small feet scurried in the cupboard. He thought he heard a creak in the corridor; he went to the door but there was no one there. From downstairs came the sound of chatter as the ratting fraternity assembled. A few barks as well as the hungry dogs were led in.

Letters begging, pleading, threatening, whining; ship's papers, references, promissory notes; even a love letter or two written in a neat, dispassionate hand. Most of the discarded documents had been spoiled; one or two were complete but probably unpaid for and therefore withheld; Blackstone wondered if the fires of ardor had died before the ink was dry on the love letters.

The man at the door said, "Put your hands up and keep them there."

Blackstone put them up.

The man said, "I don't know what you're looking for. But whatever it is I'm sure it's not there."

The man's diction was good but there was a slippery texture to it: tresses of green weed in clear water.

"Mr. Shoemark?"

"Who else? It is my room, after all."

"My name's Blackstone. I'm a Bow Street Runner. I advise you to put away your gun."

"Do you indeed?" There was femininity in his voice, too, contradicting the cruelty of his calling. Shoemark said, "I would be quite justified in shooting you, Mr. Blackstone. I find you in my room going through my papers. How am I to know you're a Bow Street Runner?"

Blackstone wondered if a man who threw snapping dogs among defenseless rats would be brave enough to shoot a man in cold blood. He turned round. Shoemark's finger tightened on the trigger of the flintlock pocket pistol in his hand. "That was very stupid of you," he said.

He was tall and thin, almost rakish. There was about him a spurious jauntiness which Blackstone had noted among the fringe members of the Fancy: yesterday's fashions, tired skin, rheumy eyes. His teeth protruded slightly, yellow and sharp; but he had no tail.

"That pistol you're holding," Blackstone said. "Bit ancient, isn't it?" He took a step forward. Shoemark jerked the gun at him. "What is it, a Ketland?"

"It's enough to blow your head off."

"I doubt it. The flint's been used too often. And at the best the hangfire between trigger pressure and explosion is too long for safety. In any case"—he lowered one hand and pointed—"it isn't cocked properly."

Shoemark lowered his eyes fractionally and Blackstone kicked, sending the pistol flying across the room. As it left his hand it fired and the ball crashed through the skylight.

Blackstone grabbed Shohmark by the lapels of his shiny, bottle-green coat and threw him on to the bed. "You might have a way with rats," he said, "but not with guns." He drew up the chair beside the bed. "And now,

79

Mr. Shoemark, I want to find a girl called Lily Spender, a client of yours I believe," hoping that the Runner Vickery, Bow Street's fraud specialist, had been right about Shoemark.

"I don't know any Lily Spender."

"I think you do." Blackstone leaned over and hit him across the face with the flat of his hand, catching him on the rebound with the back. "If you don't cooperate, I'll arrest you on a charge of being an accomplice to blackmail. You're familiar with the law, Shoemark. I'm sure you know what that entails."

"I have so many clients . . ." The weed in his voice strangled it.

"Just one, Shoemark." Then, as the thought occurred to him, "Perhaps you have the letter, Shoemark. Perhaps you're acting as more than a screever in this case. A joint enterprise, Shoemark? You acting as agent?"

"What letter? If I've written a letter for anyone then they've got it."

"Not the letter *you* wrote." Blackstone eased his chair nearer the bed. "The letter that was written to Lily Spender. The one that proves the relationship between her and a certain gentleman which makes him fair game for extortion."

Shoemark denied knowledge of any such letter.

Blackstone hit him again, then stood up and said, "All right, I'm taking you to Bow Street."

Yellow teeth nibbled. Finally Shoemark said, "All right, I know about the letter. But it's not here."

"Where is it?"

"At another premises . . ." The weed thickening.

"Then get it."

80

"Can I ask one favor?"

"You can ask."

"Everything depends on me today. There's a big crowd downstairs. No one can handle the rats like me. If I fail them they'll attack me just like a bookmaker bolting. Let me do the honors, Mr. Blackstone, and I'll find you the letter."

Blackstone agreed. He went downstairs, ordered himself a Dog's Nose and took a seat where he could keep an eye on King Rat and his subjects.

Most of the talk in the hot smoky parlor was about dogs; only a little about rats. The dogs were quiet, waiting patiently at their owner's feet or sleeping curled up in their arms. Two dogs seemed to be in charge, checking each arrival: a big old bulldog with a head like a cabbage, and a Staffordshire bull-terrier with a bitten, dangerous face.

Around the walls were prints of dogs. And stuffed dogs with rats in their mouths. One mounted six-pounder called Titch with a woman's diamante bracelet around its neck; one bulldog, with marbles for eyes and stiff shiny tongue, which had killed two hundred rats before they got their revenge and infected him with a fatal disease.

Around Blackstone sat costers in corduroy, soldiers with unbuttoned uniforms, coachmen, livery, watermen, one or two swells, a couple of barristers and a peer who was a well-known Bond Street lounger and crony of the Count d'Orsay.

At 2.35 Mellor announced that the pit was going to be lit up. As the gas flared above the white-painted circus, about six feet in diameter, with wooden walls waist-high, Shoemark made his entry with a showman's flourish, cheeks still bearing the imprint of Blackstone's hands.

The dogs, sensing the imminence of slaughter, began to wake up and bark. The spectators examined the dogs' limbs and teeth before placing bets on how many rats each could kill.

A coster from Covent Garden sat down beside Blackstone and asked, "What you doing, here, Blackie? Cricket, milling, racing, yes. But not ratting, surely."

Blackstone shrugged, pointing at the lounger who wore a Royal blue coat and a pale blue silk cravat. "It's not too degrading for him."

The coster spat. "We all know the likes of him. Getting a kick out of slumming and meeting the dangerous classes. Something to tell me lords and ladies about over dinner tonight." He gazed at the peer, curly-haired and creamy-faced. "But he'll have to watch his pockets here."

Blackstone said, "I'm watching them for him."

"I don't believe it." The coster, who was wearing his best clothes—cloth coat with contrasting lapels and red-spotted handkerchief round his neck—leaned across the table conspiratorially. "What are you really here for, Blackie?"

"A bit of sport."

"Had a bet then?"

"Not yet."

The coster lit his clay pipe. "I've got half a sovereign on the moth-eaten old terrier over there." He pointed at a vicious animal with features not unlike a rat's. "He don't look much but he's killed more rats than you've had hot dinners." He paused. "You're not listening to me, Blackie."

Blackstone stared across the small arena to the ring where the spectators leaned and jostled. One hand gripping the rim caught his notice. The nail on the thumb was long and tough, the nail of a thimble rigger.

"Excuse me." He pushed his way through the crowd; when he reached the other side there was no sign of the rigger.

"What was all that about?" the coster asked.

"Never you mind," Blackstone snapped.

A rusty cage writhing with rats was brought forward. When Shoemark approached the rats became quiet, eyes watching him trustfully. Shoemark thrust his hand into the cage and pulled them out, one by one, by their tails. Half a dozen in the first batch because a dog, a mongrel, with a clownish patch over one eye, who was being offered for sale, had to prove himself.

The six rats grouped in one spot, nose to nose, forming a quivering circle. The dog was thrown in. It sniffed the rats and walked away, embarrassed, hot on imaginary scents more appetizing than rats.

"He's a devil when he's roused," the owner announced.

But the clown wasn't to be roused. After a lot of derision he was lifted out of the ring and returned to his angry owner.

After more sales and non-sales it was time for the first match of the afternoon. This time Shoemark had to pull out fifty rats. They assembled in a heap below Blackstone and the coster. Now it was the terrier's turn to kill all of them within a stipulated period.

"I've got some side-bets," the coster confided. "Twenty-five in half the time and suchlike."

The terrier seemed to be on the coster's side. He burrowed into the heap, pulling out rat after rat, biting through their necks with one experienced snap. But he was delayed by a rat which sank its teeth into his nose and hung on.

The coster became frantic, shouting at the terrier and thumping the table with his fist.

The terrier finally shook himself free. But the delay had been too long.

Shoemark leaped over the ring and shouted, "Time."

The coster swore horribly.

One or two rats scuttled across the ring and stopped at Shoemark's feet where they began to clean themselves.

Blackstone, who felt sick, said, "So you lost half a sovereign?"

"More."

Blackstone was sympathetic. "You see that man over there?"

"What, Shoemark? Old King Rat himself?"

"Don't let him out of your sight. There's a sovereign in it if you're still with him when the sport is over."

"He'll still be here," said the coster, with surprise.

"Then it's a sovereign easily earned."

Blackstone walked into the cramped and crowded street outside which suddenly seemed as fresh as the deck of a ship.

When he returned, the sport had finished prematurely— an onslaught of canine ferocity which had exhausted supplies of rats.

Mellor was at the bar pouring spirits from the smoke-blackened barrels for the lucky gamblers and ale for the less fortunate. Of the dogs, only the Staffordshire bull-terrier and bulldog remained awake, staring suspiciously at every newcomer.

The coster was drinking hot rum in anticipation of the sovereign. Blackstone asked him the whereabouts of Shoemark.

"King Rat? He's up in his room."

Blackstone swore.

He ran up the stairs two at a time.

The door was ajar, but Blackstone barged it as if he were breaking the lock. A breeze, entering through the broken skylight, rustled the forged papers that would never be finished. . . .

King Rat had relinquished his throne. His body lay sprawled across the table, the back of his head caved in by a single blow.

The rat crouched at his feet didn't try to run away as Blackstone approached the corpse.

In his smut-brown office Sir Richard Birnie, one-time saddlemaker, favorite of the then Prince of Wales, and chief Bow Street magistrate for two years, waited for Blackstone.

He glanced at a sheaf of papers about prizefighting, a sport which held no attraction for him.

He also scanned a report by yet another committee investigating the possibility of setting up a new police force. Until last year Birnie had lit his pipe with such reports; but that was when Lord Sidmouth was Home Secretary; now Peel was in charge and everything was different.

He read with care and disgust. "Swashbuckling attitude of some Bow Street Runners . . . malpractices involving collaboration with notorious thieves . . . over-zealous methods of extracting the truth from suspects . . . patronage of taverns known to be the haunt of criminal elements . . . undue familiarity with the said rogues and payment of money thereto. . . ."

All ammunition for a Home Secretary infected with the fever for reform.

I must be firm, Birnie thought. The Runners were renowned throughout the world. Guardians of Royalty, of Parliament; captors of the cleverest murderers, thieves and confidence tricksters of the century. I must be firm. He glanced at the pictures on the wall—Henry Fielding, John Fielding the "Blind Beak" and other august predecessors—as if seeking approval.

He lit a pipe and walked to the window overlooking the gracious curve of Bow Street. Opposite stood the Brown Bear where there had been an extra cell to accommodate the overflow of felons. Through the lighted window he saw Ruthven, Page and Townshend and the serving girl with whom Blackstone consorted.

Where the hell was Blackstone?

He ordered some more tea and watched evening trying to settle in the March wind. The cries of a girl selling "Pretty pins for pretty women." A lamplighter. A band of toughs heading up West looking for trouble, any sort of trouble; brandishing their fists at the courthouse.

Birnie hoped they would be picked up by the foot patrol. If he saw those faces in court tomorrow he would be reassured that there was no necessity for a uniformed metropolitan police force.

One of the toughs barged an old man into the gutter. There was cruelty abroad. The clouds skimmed low after the departing day. Birnie, from Banff in Scotland, was glad of his house in St. Martin's Lane, with its mahogany, chintz, decanters, its servants and its big leather Bibles; and of his cottage in Acton. Glad and a little guilty.

He saw Blackstone climb out of gig. He looked at his gold repeater: the man was ten minutes late. He adopted a stern posture. But Blackstone walked straight into the Brown Bear.

"How was he killed?" Birnie asked savagely.

"Hit on the back of the head," Blackstone told him. "Could have been any weapon. A life preserver, perhaps."

"And why was he killed?"

"Because someone wanted to stop me getting that letter, I suppose."

"But no one knew you were after it."

"Sir Humphrey Cadogan did."

"He would hardly try to stop you getting it."

It wasn't very likely, Blackstone agreed. He sat opposite Birnie, the leather-topped desk between them, unsure as always of his feelings towards him. A tough old bastard certainly; but inclined to be intimidated by the authority of breeding. Once a saddlemaker always a saddlemaker. But who the hell am I?

"Perhaps Shoemark told an accomplice," Blackstone suggested.

"Then it must have been someone in that tavern. Or someone very near. Have you questioned Mellor?"

Blackstone nodded. "He never left the parlor."

Birnie re-lit his pipe and blew a jet of smoke at the portrait of Saunders Welch, the one-time High Constable of Holborn who accompanied prisoners from Newgate to Tyburn dressed all in black and riding a white horse. Started life as an apprentice trunkmaker. A good man, Welch.

The jet of smoke dispersed among the smuts and Birnie said, "Why didn't you tell me about this investigation, Blackstone?"

"I was going to, sir. Tonight as a matter of fact."

"Cadogan hasn't made a formal application for assistance from Bow Street."

"I suppose he thought it was sufficient to ask me."

"Then you should have conveyed the request to me immediately."

Blackstone conceded the point.

"Now we have a murder on our hands." Birnie watched with disapproval as Blackstone took snuff from his gold Nathaniel Mills box. A bribe? A reward? He said in his bleak moorland voice, "You had already questioned Shoemark?"

Blackstone nodded.

"And I suppose it's occurred to you that you're probably suspected of the murder? Especially as you weren't on official business."

"I suppose," Blackstone said, "that it could be described as official business as I intended to tell you about it tonight."

"I suppose so." Birnie crossed the room to the eternal fire and relit his pipe with a wooden spill. He stood, back to the flames, severe in black with a white ruff at his neck. "There are difficult times ahead, Blackstone. We have a lot of enemies." He sucked at his pipe. "I know your abilities and your value to us. . . ."

"You mean my background, sir?"

"You have a lot of contacts who are invaluable to us. A lot of knowledge of the criminal classes."

"Yes, sir," Blackstone said, remembering all those in the Rookery who regarded him as a traitor.

Birnie went on, "But your methods leave a lot to be desired. You've got to discipline yourself, Blackstone. Otherwise . . ."

"Back to the other side of the law?" He smiled faintly. "I might be invaluable there, with my contacts at Bow Street and my knowledge of the Runners' methods."

"It's the future of the Runners I'm concerned with," Birnie said, pointing the smoke-dribbling stem of his pipe at Blackstone. "Your behavior is ammunition to our enemies." He went to the desk and picked up the report of the committee. "Ill-treatment of suspects—that's one of the accusations. Did you hit this man Shoemark at all?"

"Not hard," Blackstone said.

"Did anyone see you?"

"No, sir."

"Or hear you?"

"Only a few rats," Blackstone said.

Finally, Birnie got around to the original purpose of the summons. He picked up the sheaf of papers on prize-fighting.

"A reprehensible pastime," he said.

"A very popular one, sir."

"Popularity is no yardstick. Badger-baiting is popular. You don't condone that, do you, Blackstone?"

Blackstone shook his head. "The badger has no choice. The fighters do."

"I wonder." Birnie examined his cold fingers. "Do you know of a single fighter who has emerged from the upper classes?"

"Not offhand," Blackstone said.

"Exactly. Men go in for prizefighting to get enough money to claw themselves out of the cesspit of their lives. Coalheavers taking home fifteen shillings a week, plumbers dying from the effects of white lead, Irish navvies quartered in tents beside the canals." He paused, staring at

89

Blackstone. "Jews who can't get work and Negroes who can't buy an apprenticeship because they haven't got the money."

Blackstone stared back at him, wondering. He said, "The most depraved pastime of all is watching a public hanging."

"Maybe." Birnie thumbed the sheaf of papers. "At the moment I'm concerned with prizefighting. The boxers are being exploited and brutalized by the patrons—and the Fancy as they choose to call themselves. They are being paid to injure, maim and sometimes kill each other for the sadistic pleasure of a bloodthirsty crowd. Can that be right, Blackstone? Isn't it far worse in its way than unpremeditated murder? A crime of passion?"

Blackstone didn't reply.

"If it is such a noble art why don't the more privileged citizens take part?"

"They do, sir," Blackstone said without conviction.

"Ah yes, in the Fives Court. Wearing gloves."

"Boxing is changing," Blackstone said. "It's becoming more skillful. Soon the old slogging match will be a thing of the past."

"I doubt it," Birnie said. "I doubt it very much. The Fancy"—contempt in his voice—"want blood and bruises not skill." He tossed Blackstone a copy of *The Times* with a passage marked in pencil. "Have you read that?"

It was a report of a case from Buckingham Assizes in which a fighter had been charged with "feloniously killing and slaying" his opponent. The report included some colorful details of a brain hemorrhage.

Blackstone said, "I see he was found not guilty."

"Quite rightly so. He wasn't the murderer."

"The Fancy was, I suppose?"

Birnie nodded. "Have you ever attended a fight, Black-stone?"

"If you remember, sir, I recovered the diamond ring stolen from Prince Esterhazy at Moulsey. It was, I believe, a present from the Emperor of Prussia," he added, en-listing the support of Birnie's reverence for aristocracy.

But Birnie was in inexorable mood. "That was in a professional capacity. . . ." But before he could continue Blackstone elaborated, "A prizefight is rather like a flash tavern. You know where to find the villains. I guarantee that at any fight I can find half a dozen wanted men, apart from petty criminals, that is."

Birnie gazed at him speculatively, rubbing his hands together like a forester rubbing sticks to make fire.

After rubbing away for a while without ignition he said, "This trial of the prizefighter has caused quite a stir in some circles."

"Among the reformers?"

"Yes, Blackstone, among the reformers. You sound as if you've consigned them to the criminal classes."

"Not at all, sir. I'm well aware of the need for reform." He gestured towards the bright, star-spangled, criminal night. "Right on our doorstep. Workhouses, factories, lodging houses. . . . It merely seems to me that the re-formers have their priorities wrong."

"It's a matter of opinion," Birnie said. He picked up the other sheaf of papers. "The fact remains that rioting and the incidence of crime at prizefights has been put forward as evidence of the need for a new police force. Further-more"—he appraised Blackstone once more—"it is alleged that some Bow Street Runners actively support prize-fighting."

"Good God!" Blackstone exclaimed.

91

"I'm glad you're suitably shocked." Birnie leaned forward. "Under the Act of 1750, Blackstone, prizefighting is illegal. We're going to enforce that law. We're going to stop prizefighting."

"I see," Blackstone said.

"And I'm putting you in charge of the campaign to stamp it out."

8

Blackstone's crusade against prizefighting had two immediate results: it increased the numbers of his enemies and it brought him closer to Laura Cadogan.

He started by making known his intentions in the citadels of the Fancy. Firstly at the Pugilistic Club—its 120 members all from the country's top "ten thousand"— which was determined to stamp out the fixing of fights.

In the committee room he met two titled members who spared him some of their time. They exuded breeding.

Blackstone attacked, conscious of sharp angles in his speech and flamboyant flourishes of his dress.

He sat awkwardly on a fragile chair and pointed out that, although the intentions of the club were laudable, the sport they patronized was illegal.

Sir Henry Bathurst, Bt., austere and honest, said, "Edmund Blackstone, isn't it? Read about you. Something to do with a riot in Dublin, wasn't it?"

Blackstone said it was.

Sir Arthur Willoughby, belligerent and honest, with a history of apoplectic scenes in clubs, said, "Not a Catholic, are you?"

Blackstone said he wasn't a Catholic. Nor a Protestant.

"Catholic emancipation," Willoughby growled, consigning all manifestations of equality to the gallows.

Blackstone placed his baton on the table between them. "Religion aside, gentlemen, the fact remains that prizefighting is against the law."

Bathurst said, "An obsolete law. As you know, Blackstone, prizefighting has royal patronage. The present King was a great enthusiast. And the Duke of Clarence, of course. I remember him arriving late for dinner at Brighton because he'd been to see the 'Game of Chicken,' Henry Pearce you know"—looking quizzically at Blackstone to see if he did know—"fight Gully." He fingered his cold-looking nose. "I don't imagine that Birnie would want to upset the Royal family, would he?"

"When the King was Prince of Wales," Blackstone said, "he arranged a fight between Mendoza and Sam Martin. It didn't prevent the 10th Regiment of the Dragoons breaking it up. And you may recall," he went on, turning to Willoughby, "that the King largely withdrew his support when he saw a fight between Tyne and Earl which resulted in Earl's death."

Baronet and knight were quiet for a moment.

"You seem to know a lot about it," Willoughby snapped. "Have you read it up?" Blackstone interpreted this as: *If you fellows can read.*

Bathurst, the more dangerous of the two in his donnish way, asked, "Why is Birnie suddenly so concerned about prizefighting? Could it be anything to do with Peel? A sort of diversionary tactic as it were? What do you think, Blackstone?"

"It's not for me to say."

"No," Bathurst said, "I suppose it isn't."

"Although," Blackstone said, "I imagine that he is acting with obvious reasons."

"Which are?"

"Prizefighting encourages rioting and corrupt practices."

"You sound like a clergyman," Willoughby said, lighting a stubby, belligerent pipe, "not a Bow Street Runner. Why not stop racing and cricket? Close down the Jockey Club and the Marylebone Cricket Club. There's more rioting at cricket, dammit, than prizefighting. What about when Leicester beat Coventry? There was a battle after that."

"That was over thirty years ago," Blackstone said, confidence returning.

"By God but you really know your sport, don't you?" Bathurst gazed at Blackstone through Willoughby's smoke. "Are you a member of the Fancy, Blackstone?"

You had to admire Bathurst; but he was, after all, a barrister. Blackstone said, "No, sir. Although I've been to some fights in the course of my duties."

"Do you know a fellow called Foley?"

"A little."

"Says he knows you quite well."

Blackstone shrugged.

"Basking in your glory, eh, Blackstone?"

"If you say so, Sir Henry."

An impatient jet of smoke from Willoughby. "What do you intend to do?"

"I shall take the appropriate steps to break up every fight I hear about. Warn the magistrates, attend personally, call in the military if necessary. I thought it only courteous to warn you gentlemen of my intentions." He stood up to leave.

95

Bathurst held up his hand. "You know, Blackstone, it is the declared aims of the Pubilistic Club to further the more decent aspects of the sport. To stop fights being crossed and to provide purses so that penniless but promising young men can fight without falling into unscrupulous hands?"

"I'm aware of that," Blackstone said.

"Doesn't that impress you?"

"It impresses me," Blackstone told him. "But I would be more impressed if you had the standing of the Jockey Club."

Their indignation continued to afford him pleasure as he headed for the Daffy Club where his warning was received mutinously. At the Fives Court it was at first received with disbelief, then anger by the majority; although a few thought the gloved sparring matches at the Fives Court might benefit.

When Blackstone arrived at the Court, declining to pay the "three bobs" entrance, there was a benefit match in progress between a retiring Birmingham fighter—Birmingham second only to Bristol as a breeding ground for boxers—and a younger fighter, an Irish coalheaver, who was allowing himself to get the worst of it. They fought without animosity, gloves drawing a little blood now and again.

Most of the Fancy stood around the four-foot-high ring, elegant in their raffish way, applauding with restraint. The old boxer had brawled his way to fame, and the niceties of exhibition boxing came awkwardly to him.

There had been too many benefits this year; too many bouts in which the result was academic; too much sparring which blunted the killer instincts of the fighters for the open-air spectacles when true sportsmen expected to see fighters batter each other into insensibility.

Several spectators left when Blackstone arrived, mostly pickpockets. Which pleased Blackstone because the presence of the Runner Page, who specialized in "dippers," hadn't frightened them.

Page, fingers fluttering, said, "What are you doing here, Blackie?" And then, words as crafty as his fingers, "I didn't know you supported this sort of thing?"

"I'm here to stop it," Blackstone said.

"Oh yes," Page said with disbelief.

"On Birnie's instructions."

"Oh yes," Page said with belief. "You won't be very popular. Down here or up there." He pointed up at the windows of the dressing-roome where nobility, and occasionally Royalty, gathered above the ring in the lofty court.

"I'm not very popular now," Blackstone said, thinking that Page owned all the deeds of unpopularity. "There, why don't you do something about him?" He pointed at a pickpocket passing a wallet to his accomplice, the stickman.

Page grabbed the accomplice. But, it seemed to Blackstone, with reluctance. He wondered if Page had a pick of these pickings. Anything was possible with someone as pallidly self-righteous as Page.

Blackstone moved round the ring confiding his assignment, leaving behind a wake of astonishment.

In one corner, beside an Italian painter daubing cadmium-red blood on his canvas, he found Foley, as elegant as a moulting cagebird.

Foley greeted him wanly. He pointed at the two boxers trying to do pretty things with their brawling bodies. "I'll give you . . ."

"Six to four," Blackstone said. "I shouldn't worry—it's a foregone conclusion."

Foley retreated into his threadbare topcoat which had cost a lot of money a long time ago. He had gambled and lost his home and his wife's affection, and it was less than even money that tonight he would be bound for the twopenny lodging houses of the "Holy Land" of St. Giles Rookery, or some other slum hidden by the imposing shadows of the mansions of St. George's or Marylebone.

Blackstone gave him a sovereign.

"Thank you, Blackie. I've a feeling my luck will change."

"I'm glad."

"Blackie."

"Yes?"

"What's all this I hear about a lot of blunt going on the fight between Houseman and the black boy?"

"It seems that some swell has put £5,000 on Houseman. God knows who. There's enough of them ready to throw their money around. Especially those who haven't got it. Lord Blandford, perhaps. I don't know if he's a betting man but he's a spender, the money-lender's friend. He paid £500 for a shrub from Lee and Kennedy's the other day."

"But why on Houseman, Blackie? Everyone reckons the black boy's favorite to win. It's only this big bet keeping the prices fairly even." His sad face pleaded. "Do you know anything, Blackie? Any point in wagering a little something on Houseman?"

A blob of blood from the Birmingham fighter's nose landed on the artists's canvas. Thoughtfully, he enlarged it with cadmium.

Blackstone said, "Why should I know anything?"

"I just thought you might. You meet a lot of people who know about these things." His unhappy face looked knowing. Or is it my imagination, Blackstone wondered.

Foley went on, "It's funny we should both have been together at Hungerford the day the black boy made a fool out of Hansom. That was the beginning for him, I shouldn't wonder. Now they say Sir Humphrey Cadogan's backing him."

"Then he's in good hands."

"He must be good if the Cad's taken an interest."

The Irish boxer fell with a thump, then clambered up making theatrical gestures of admiration at the old fighter's prowess.

Blackstone didn't reply and Foley said, "They say Donnelly's not managing him. That's odd, isn't it, Blackie?"

"Perhaps the Negroes want to keep him to themselves." Blackstone said. "Why don't you ask Bill Richmond in his pub next door?"

"I will." Was it slyness on his face?

Blackstone said, "I hear you've been talking to some members of the Pugilistic Club."

"I may have been," Foley said.

'Rather exalted company for you, isn't it? With respect," he added.

"I wasn't always like this, Blackie."

"I know that. I'm sorry." The bout came to an end to the accompaniment of cheerful applause from the connoisseurs who remembered the Birmingham fighter's moment of glory when he won a prizefight almost unconscious on his feet after fifty rounds. "Bathurst, wasn't it, that you were talking to?"

"Bathurst?"

"Sir Henry Bathurst from the Pugilistic Club that you were talking to the other day?"

Foley nodded vaguely. "I believe it was. I met him at a

fight at Coombe Wood. He remembered me," he said, as if it were an accolade.

"Did he ask you about me?"

"He just said he'd seen us together. I said I'd known you for a long time. That's all. Why, is there anything wrong, Blackie?"

No, Blackstone assured him, there was nothing wrong.

"That's good, Blackie. I wouldn't want to say anything that might harm you. We've been friends for a long time, haven't we?"

Blackstone slipped him another sovereign. "Just one thing," he said. "Always remember that I only attend fights in an official capacity."

"I'll remember, Blackie."

Blackstone left him to lose the two sovereigns on a fight, a race, a cock-fight, a game of cards or the number of grains of sand on the seashore.

While he toured the haunts of the Fancy letting it be known that he was authorized to lead the campaign against prizefighting, Blackstone applied himself to another task: training Ebony Joe for his fight with Billy the Butcher in a month's time.

He ran with him across the fields at dawn when the mist still hung low in the milky light and they were alone; and again at dusk as the mist regrouped and the only spectators were the stirring night animals. He turned the spare room into a small gymnasium? he fed his protégé with steaks, milk, eggs and vegetables. He taught him footwork; he cautioned him to use speed and agility to avoid punishment—and to hell with the Fancy who wanted blood and bruises.

Occasionally Ebony left Paddington—to see his old father, he claimed.

And all the time he reacted to Blackstone's help with a mixture of gratitude and resentment. "Why are you doing this for me? I just don't understand it."

"Perhaps you will, one day," Blackstone replied. Perhaps.

The day after Blackstone's visit to the Fives Court he met Laura Cadogan at a soirée given by the Lady Cork at her home in Old Burlington Street.

The old countess always invited a contrasting assortment of guests to her evenings: Members of Parliament, the noble and the ignoble, wits, dandies, aristocratic simpletons—often Georgian offspring—clergymen, spies, poets, artists and playwrights.

Long before the death of King Rat, Blackstone had been engaged to protect the guests from thieves. As usual he went straight to Sol's Tavern in Drury Lane to warn the cracksmen who gathered there to give the party a wide berth.

The flash patrons, who were playing cards and tossing for sovereigns at the end of the bar reserved for them, regarded him sardonically and invited him to buy them drinks.

Jack Barclay, a burglar who owned his own hackney carriage with a racehorse between the shafts to speed him away from him crimes, said, "What if we don't stay away from the party, Blackie?"

Blackstone supped a pot of ale. "For one thing," he said, "your highly satisfactory way of life will come to an end."

"Such threats," murmured deaf Ben Brain, the owner of a swarm of pickpockets, who seemed to hear more than most.

"And you'd lose a lot of contacts," Barclay said. "A lot

of information, Blackie. Where would you go to then? A ratting tavern in Soho, maybe?"

"Maybe," Blackstone said.

"We'd better watch ourselves," Brain said. "We hear that the last person you questioned died rather suddenly."

"A bit extreme, wasn't it, Blackie?" Barclay said. "After all he can't answer your questions now, can he?" His hand strayed to a diamond pin in his cravat.

Brain, hand cupped to his ear, pockets tight and small to discourage his employees, said, "Doing a bit of blackmail, was he, Blackie?" He tossed for a sovereign and won it. "He was only a cheap little screever, Blackie. Why bother?"

Barclay said, "Perhaps Blackie sees the hand of Henry Challoner in it."

The possibility had occurred to Blackstone, but he had rejected it. Blackmail wasn't a crime applauded by Challoner, the only man to escape justice after the Cato Street Conspiracy: the cleverest criminal in London: born, like Blackstone, in St. Giles Rookery, of uncertain fatherhood. Perhaps even the same father—paternity was as accidental as pollination in the creaking nocturnal slums.

Barclay, dark and flash and handsome, seemed too self-satisfied, Blackstone decided. He took a copy of *Hue and Cry* from his pocket. "Been to Cirencester lately, Jack?" He ran his finger down the column of stolen property. "Some good plate pinched there last week."

Barclay grinned, but not too readily. "What of it, culley?"

"Some of it turned up at the Sugar Loaf near here. We traced it back and got a good description of the cracksman. Seems he escaped with a hackney and a very fast horse. . . ."

102

Barclay bought a round of drinks. "All right," he said "We'll leave the good countess's guests alone."

She wore blue, of course, tight against her breasts, high up her neck. She was at ease with everyone and Blackstone envied her.

"So we're allies now," she said, sipping champagne. She stood close to him. "Both sworn to end the depravity."

Blackstone stared at the bubbles spiraling in his glass.

"Well, we are, aren't we?"

"It would seem so."

"I misjudged you. I suppose it was because you looked so much like a prizefighter." The scar apologized. "Your build, I mean, not your face." She looked doubtful. "Did you ever do any fighting, Blackie?"

"A little," he said. "As a boy. To survive," he added.

"I understand," she said, gracious with her knowledge of the dangerous classes.

"Do you?"

"Of course I do."

"You say you've been in the slum?"

"You don't doubt me, do you?"

"I don't doubt you. But I think it's odd. Why weren't you attacked?"

"One day," she said mysteriously—and a little tipsily—I'll let you into the secret." She leaned against him momentarily, then recoiled. "Do you know most of the people here?"

"Some of them."

She began to point out the titled on the assumption that Blackstone only knew the commoners. There was Lord Alvanley, one of London's wits. A jolly corpulent man with dark hair and a small nose from which snuff escaped on to his upper lip. His dinners, at Park Street and Melton, Laura said, were the finest in the land. But his recklessness with money was legendary. Did Blackstone know that he spent a small fortune in keeping an apricot tart on his sideboard all the year round? Blackstone, thinking of children scavenging Covent Garden for rotten plums, said he hadn't heard.

She pointed out Lord Petersham, renowned for his individual habits. He refused to leave his house until 6 p.m., his carriages and coachmen's livery were all brown (because, it was said, he had once been in love with a woman called Brown) and he had the finest collection of blends of tea—Pekoe, Souchong, Bohea, Russian—in London.

Petersham strolled over, a light-blue Sèvres snuff-box in his hand. "Blackstone, isn't it?" He spoke with a slight lisp. "I've read about you. I hear you're here to prevent thieves stealing *objets d'art* such as this." He fondled the snuff-box.

Blackstone said, "Is that your property, sir?"

Petersham said, "Of course it is."

"That's all right then," Blackstone told him. "I just wanted to be sure."

Petersham smiled uncertainly before lisping away.

"You don't have much respect, do you, Blackie?"

"I respect anyone who deserves it."

"Do you respect my father?"

"If he deserves it."

"I don't respect him."

"I gathered that."

"That's why I'm trying to get away. But it's very difficult for a girl. . . ."

"Not so difficult," Blackstone said.

"You don't know. It's a man's world. . . ."

Blackstone accepted more champagne. The gaslight shone on her thick ringlets. The champagne had colored her cheeks, the scar was smiling.

He said more gently, "At least you're trying." She was living with a widow who had been a friend of her mother in Hanover Square. She went daily to a building in Clerkenwell where each room was a cubicle of philanthropy and zeal.

Blackstone said, "Are you the only person dealing with prizefighting reforms?"

She nodded. "I'm the only woman there. Everyone else is more concerned with other reforms. Prisons, opium, treadmills and things like that."

"Isn't anyone applying themselves to the exploitation of children?"

"They may be."

"But only you involved with prizefighting. . . ." Suspicions formed in his mind. "Have you contributed much money to this society?"

"A little."

"I thought so." He drained his glass of champagne. "Soon, thanks to you and your father, England should be a better place to live in. Unless," he added, "you happen to be a child living in St. Giles."

Their affinity shrank.

She said coolly, "Do you know that man over there?"

Blackstone gazed across the elegant, high-ceilinged room bubbling with champagne chatter, and saw Townshend, the most famous Bow Street Runner. "Yes," he said, "I know him."

"I thought *you* were here to protect property."

"So did I," Blackstone said.

Blackstone respected Townshend; admired him too—his exploits, his contacts, his money. There were many stories told about Townshend.

Such as the time he had been escort on a carriage taking a large sum of money to Reading. He had taken with him Joseph Manton, the gunmaker, and at Hounslow they were stopped by three footpads. Manton was about to shoot when Townshend stopped him, saying, "Let me talk to these gentlemen." The familiar sound of Townshend's voice, it was said, so scared the footpads that they fled.

Townshend was invited to attend most state functions; he became friendly with Royalty, the Prime Minister, the Duke of Wellington, most of the Cabinet and the nobility. In his time he had taken more thieves than any other Runner; but that time was in the past.

He was short and plump and, out of doors, wore his own uniform: kerseymere breeches, blue straightcut coat, broadbrimmed white hat.

He greeted Blackstone amiably. "Blackstone," he said. "Good to see you." He grinned. "There'll be the devil to pay if anything happens tonight with both of us here."

The devil to pay for me, Blackstone thought. He looked for the cunning and the courage; saw only a plump, middle-aged man, glossy with good living. But he had been tough all right; now, he was like a woman letting herself go as she unlaced her corset.

Blackstone said, "I didn't realize you were going to be here as well."

"No reason why you should," Townshend assured him.

He squeezed his arm. "No reason at all. I pop up all over the place these days. As a matter of fact the Countess invited me personally—as a friend, you know."

"No," Blackstone said, "I didn't know."

They were interrupted by Lord Petersham. He said as urgently as his lisp permitted, "I've been robbed." He accused Blackstone and appealed to Townshend.

Townshend said, "What have you lost?"

"A purse. It was in my coat in the ante-room."

Blackstone started towards the ante-room, but Townshend stopped him. "Anyone else been robbed I wonder," he said.

Blackstone examined the guests: not a villain to be seen. He said to Petersham, "Are you sure it was in your coat?"

"Of course I'm sure. What are you going to do about it?"

Within five minutes one peer and one baronet reported thefts from the ante-room.

Blackstone said, "We'd better search everyone."

Townshend sighed. "It really is too bad of her," he said. He crossed the room and spoke to the hostess, the Countess of Cork.

When he returned he told Blackstone, "The property will be returned within a couple of minutes." He allowed his glass to be refilled. "She can't help herself, poor dear. She invited me to protect her guests against herself. But she means no harm," he added.

The house in Hanover Square was tall and discreet with a fanlight above the door and a brass knocker in the shape of a lion's claw.

The owner was away for the week. A fire blazed in the drawing-room and a lady's-maid was waiting up to tend to Laura.

Blackstone said, "Tell her to go to bed."

Laura Cadogan shivered despite the heat of the fire. "And you?" she said.

"I'll stay."

Laura told the maid to go; she curtsied away to report developments below stairs.

Blackstone kissed Laura on the lips. She hardly responded and he stroked her hair. "You know," she said, "I've always found this sort of thing rather distasteful. Ever since . . ."

"But that was a long time ago."

"I can't help it," she said.

"You can't go on like this."

"Why not?" She stood away from him, firelight leaping around her. "A lot of women marry and have children but they never have any pleasure."

"Not the women I know."

"You're very brutal. So like a lot of my father's friends. And yet in many ways you're so gentle."

"And you haven't awoken yet."

"I don't think I want to." She flared a little. "You're do damn sure of yourself."

Blackstone shook his head. "That shows how little you know. I nearly made a fool of myself earlier this evening. Only Townshend saved me."

Laura said, "That wasn't your fault. He should have told you before."

She cares, Blackstone thought. But do I? How much of her attraction was her unwillingness? The unmelted core contradicting her body: hips, breast, the slur in her voice,

108

the Swiss-peasant hair. The challenge, egotism, aggrieved masculinity.

He said, "Some day you'll have to. Why not now?"

"So subtle," she said. "Such a subtle man." She tried to control her shivering.

"It's not cold," he said.

"And the future?" she asked, warming her hands in front of the flaming, autumn-smelling logs. "What of the future when you've been victorious yet again?"

He grinned. "We are crusaders together."

"And the other girls. What about them. Isn't there one particular girl?"

"Not one particular girl," he told her. "Scores of them."

He picked her up and carried her up the stairs to her bedroom.

Much later Blackstone lay thoughtfully in the big bed and considered his victory. Pyrrhic. Was that the word?

Laura Cadogan lay beside him, naked body somehow more slumbrously satisfied than it had any right to be. She was drifting into sleep; but every now and again she opened her eyes and gazed at him steadily.

It had been the first time; of that there was no doubt. And yet there was experience, as if the instincts had been tutored inside the dormant body. Even now as her hand stretched out to him . . . and returned disappointed.

They were, he decided, the most beautiful breasts he had ever seen; the rightful property of the woman she had just become.

Blackstone the victor bent and kissed the scar for the first time. "I've wanted to do that ever since I met you," he told her. "I know," she said, gazing at him steadily.

9

The fight with Blackstone had been inevitable, Ebony Joe decided afterwards. For one thing he resented the rigors of training; for another he wanted more money, and he wanted it quickly.

With cash lent to him by Blackstone, Ebony put his father in a clean room in Camden Town. A room with a fire and a bed, an easy chair, rugs, crockery and a few books which neither of them could read.

But the old man with the hair like sooty smoke and the creased, gum-snapping face was unsettled by the cleanliness and respectability around him, regarding both with deep suspicion.

Walking away from the Daffy Club one day after meeting Donnelly, Ebony found the old man begging on the roadside, his shapeless hat and old placard about being a victim of the slave trade—written for threepence by a failed screever—in front of him.

Ebony Joe had no fixed beliefs about stealing. But his views on begging were decided . . .

When he was three years old Ebenezer Kentucky's father positioned him on the fringe of the Rookery near a

111

missionary society. He was half-clothed and taught to cultivate a graveyard cough; the blackness of his shivering limbs accentuated his alien plight, and for a while he did very well as well-dressed men and women with pulpit faces paused outside the missionary building, throwing him coppers and murmuring, "Poor little blackbird."

But the other gegors became resentful when they realized that Ebenezer's misery was more piteous than their sores manufactured from soap and vinegar, their fits produced with the aid of soap under the tongue, their wounds simulated by cuts of meat bandaged to their limbs.

He was driven away with kicks and cudgels and his father was severely cautioned by the scandalized leaders of the begging profession.

While his father stayed on his old pitch—not offering much competition because the philanthropy of the wealthy rarely extended to the aged—Ebenezer was dispatched barefoot around the houses begging for old clothes, which could be sold at the dollyshops, and old shoes—displaying his blistered heels.

During this apprenticeship Ebenezer met many types of gegors. Blind beggars with their dogs; beggars claiming to be victims of the latest sea disaster or pit accident; beggars specializing in accosting clergymen; children hired out at threepence a day by deprived parents to beggar bands; and the élite of the medicants—those with elaborate begging letters and starving dependants to prove their claims.

For a time Ebenezer carried a letter. It read (so he was told):

> For God's sake help this poor black wafe instantly. His father is dying from the horrible wounds inflicted by the whips of the American slave-drivers. His mother has long since departed. A few shillings could

help this child who has recently recovered from the ravages of newmonia to assure himself of a future in this blessed land. Please be merciful. On his bended nees the riter of this letter asks God to bless you for your charity.

The letter moved many butlers to dispatch Ebenezer with a kick up the backside.

Without protest his father allowed himself to be taken back to Camden Town by hackney. (The drive showing reluctance to transport a beggar until Ebony thrust his knuckles into his windpipe.)

Ebony lectured the old man severely, demanding to know where his pride was. His father peered back through the goveling years and confessed that he didn't know.

Ebony strutted through the white-washed room, rattled the crockery, tested the bed and, thanks to Blackstone, managed to read the titles of a couple of books.

The old man looked at him impassively.

"You make me sick," Ebony told him.

The gums worked, yellowing eyes blinked.

"I find you a decent drum and what do you do—go back on the streets."

His father seemed to be grinning, but it was only the way the wrinkles had set—half-way between please and thanks.

Ebony brewed some tea. They drank it, as if sealing a bond, and Ebony gave his father more money than he could afford.

At first there was freshness on the skyline, then light, then a pink flush without warmth. You imagined you could smell dew, and the warm smell of a bakery because you were so hungry. The cows in their sheds slept on; a formation of geese made an arrowhead for the day.

They loped across a field, breath smoking energetically. Ebony didn't know how Blackstone managed it because he was at least thirty. Because he was a Bow Street *Runner*, he decided. *Ha Ha*. But he resented the older man's fitness. There was injustice about it somewhere: there was always injustice somewhere.

Ebony lengthened his stride, but Blackstone kept ahead.

Ebony stopped at a stile. "Can't we give it a rest?" he asked, panting.

"Another mile yet," Blackstone said; although his breath wasn't coming too easily.

"I think you're overdoing it. I bet Houseman isn't slogging himself to death like this."

"I shouldn't imagine he is. He'll be as agile as a carthorse when you fight him."

"And I'll be as weak as an old dray on its way to the knacker's yard."

"With all that steak inside you? Nonsense."

They wore thin vests, cotton drawers and woolen stockings. Ebony felt the sweat cooling. The sun rose higher, setting fire to islands of cloud.

They started to run again, on the home stretch to Paddington village.

There was a small pain in Ebony's chest, a needle sewing a stitch in his side.

What if I did take the money offered by Donnelly? No one would ever know. I could see the old man right for the rest of his life (which wasn't long). And in any case I need the money right now: the dollymop who claimed she was

114

in trouble; the money lost on the cock-fight last night when he'd told Blackstone he was visiting his father.

What do I owe Blackstone? He's in it for the brass, the glory. What else?

I wouldn't be the first boxer, Ebony assured himself, to lose my first fight and then punch my way to the championship. And I'd have money in my pockets; enough to buy a few wets, treat a few girls, back a few horses. A change from training all day on steak, milk and early morning dew.

He could, he supposed, ask Blackstone for more money. But that would be begging. Compared with begging, cheating was almost noble.

Instead of stripping off, washing and dressing while the tea brewed Blackstone lingered in the improvised gymnasium. He looked as if he were measuring it up.

Ebony took the opportunity to voice his grievances again: over-training, too much discipline. Not enough money he implied—without asking for more.

Blackstone swung a pair of gloves. "Sorry for yourself, aren't you?" he said.

"I'm not being treated fairly," Ebony said, watching the swing of the gloves.

"I think you're being treated very fairly. You wanted to be spotted that day at Hungerford, didn't you, Ebony?"

Ebony said he did.

"And you got yourself a patron. But not quite the sort you wanted. Not just a rich man who would put up the blunt and not give a pennyworth of cold gin what damage you took as long as you won. As long as you were still on your feet when some poor old bruiser couldn't take any more. That's all they would have been worried about." Blackstone paused. "You looked good that day, Ebony. You had potential. But not the stuff of champions in the eyes of the men with the money. They want sloggers not stylists."

"I'm both," Ebony said.

"You've got a big head," Blackstone said. "An easy target for Houseman.

"I could lick Houseman with one hand behind my back."

"That's not what one man with a lot of money to wager thinks." Blackstone stopped swinging the gloves and stared at Ebony. "Do you know anything about it?"

"I know someone's supposed to have put £5,000 on Houseman," Ebony said, gazing at the daffodils in the gardens across the street. "They must be soft in the head."

"That's all you know?"

"Why *should* I know anything else?" He sought initiative. 'Why don't you put some blunt on Houseman, Mr. Blackstone? You don't seem to think much of my chances."

"If you carry on training like this I will."

"Strike me blind!" Ebony said. "Every morning and evening out running. Walking in the day. Working out in the gym. Eating steaks, drinking milk . . . and a little ale. What do you want with me?"

"I want you to stay away from dollymops," Blackstone said, smiling a little.

"What dollymops?"

"Dollymops like the one you were flexing your muscle with last night. The one you were boozing with in the Horse and Dolphin next door to the Fives Court."

"I didn't see you there."

116

"I wasn't there."

"Then how do you know about her?"

"London's my parish," Blackstone said.

Ebony thought: You smug bastard.

Blackstone went on, "No more dollymops, Ebony. Not before the fight anyway. No more hot gin," he added, "and no more money down the pit at cock-fights. You can't afford it, Ebony."

Ebony said, "I can do without you. I did for Hansom, didn't I? And I'll do for Houseman, too. I'm going to be a champion, Mr. Blackstone. And I can do it without you but you can't do without me."

"Why's that, Ebony?"

Ebony Joe faltered. For some time he had been aware of a mysterious quality in Blackstone's attitude. He suspected that it might be kindness, and this made him uneasy.

"Why's that, Ebony?"

"Because you want to be there when I collect the glory. I reckon you want a slice of that, Mr. Blackstone. And a slice of the blunt."

"Ah," Blackstone murmured.

"Well, don't you?"

"Perhaps, Ebony." He was putting the gloves on. "Although it's hardly likely because I would be sacked from Bow Street if it became known that I was backing you. You know that—you threatened me with it once."

You couldn't retreat, never retreat. Ebony said, "It would be different if we made a lot of brass, wouldn't it? You wouldn't care about the Runners then."

"I would," Blackstone said. He punched gloved fists together. "So you think you're ready to take all-comers, do you, Ebony?"

117

Ebony felt confidence return, saw Hansom's face dodging into his fist. He breathed deeply, feeling the play of his muscles, the agility and anticipation curled inside him. He nodded. "Almost anyone. Not the top six," he conceded. "Not yet."

"I'll do a deal with you," Blackstone said. "I'll fight you now. If you win you can have it your way. Girls, booze . . . whatever you like. I'll stick behind you. But if I win you do it my way. How does that appeal to you?"

Ebony stared at his thirty-year-old patron, who had probably been boozing and womanizing for fifteen years or more. Fit for his age—certainly. But the speed would have gone, the stamina. And he had never been trained to fight. I am Ebony Joe, the black hope of England. Future champion.

Ebony shrugged. "As you like. . . ."

Blackstone grinned and threw him a pair of gloves. "Don't worry about hurting me."

"I won't," Ebony said.

Blackstone closed the door and glanced around the room, bare except for dumb-bells, a couple of mats and a bag filled with wet sawdust which Blackstone had hung up for Ebony to punch. "Just about the right size," he said. "Are you ready?" Ebony said he was and Blackstone said, "Right. Up to scratch then."

Ebony thought Blackstone adopted too stiff a pose. He saw the first blow coming, slowly it seemed. He took in on his left, but hesitated, finding to his surprise that he was reluctant to counter-punch his mentor.

Never hesitate. Blackstone caught him with a right, stinging his ear. Very well, Ebony thought. If he means business then he'd better watch out. The blow on the ear had been a little treacherous; but slow and lacking power.

Ebony feinted with his left, swung with his right. But,

118

with a lucky maneuver, Blackstone parried it. Poor old Hansom hadn't been so lucky. Ebony did some pretty things, swaying, ducking, moving his feet—and received a thump on the nose.

"A little claret there," Blackstone said.

Ebony shook his head as a trickle of blood emerged from his nostrils.

"Keep your guard up," Blackstone said, making his point by landing a blow high on Ebony's chest.

Ebony felt his temper rising. He punched a little wildly. Blackstone bobbed and swayed with an agility surprising in a man of his age. Also he back-pedaled so that Ebony, carried forward by the impetus of his wasted blows, stumbled.

Blackstone looked at the open target and shook his head. "I couldn't," he said.

Ebony sniffed up blood, brushing his nose with his glove. "Come on," he said. "Why don't you have a go?"

Blackstone's glove caught him full in the face. Before I'd finished speaking, Ebony thought. Treachery again. The bastard. The smug bastard.

Ebony gathered his natural skills and new knowledge into a black parcel of hatred. Careful, canny, fists bobbing. But Blackstone was moving too, quicker than anyone Ebony had fought before. And Ebony realized that Blackstone was the first man he'd fought who didn't just slog, butt, grapple . . . He was faced with his own skills.

Ebony got home a couple of blows, heard the breath punched out of Blackstone's lungs, saw him wince. But no claret. He sniffed up his own blood, watching Blackstone's eyes for messages. Get him swaying the wrong way by feinting with the right, then two swift lefts, close in, all the weight of the body behind them.

At that moment Blackstone made the same move.

119

Ebony swayed. Realized it was the wrong way. Too late. Two lefts cracked him in the face. He went down, blood spattering his vest. Leapt to his feet and took a blow on the chin that pole-axed him.

Blackstone said, "That's enough lad." His voice was gentle. "We don't want to damage you too much before your fight with Houseman."

"I'll fight on," Ebony said, spraying blood around.

"I shouldn't. You did well enough. Nothing to feel ashamed of."

Ebony stood up on bending, sapling legs, and went after Blackstone.

Blackstone stepped aside and gave him a half-hearted clout which was enough to put him down again.

"Another time," Ebony said, head between his knees. "A return match."

"You remember your promise to train my way?"

Ebony nodded between his knees.

"Then I'll make some tea." While they drank it Blackstone said, "Promise me one more thing, Ebony."

"What's that?"

"Never lose your temper while you're milling." He finished his tea. "And now we'll run another mile. You're too slow by half."

Ebony met Donnelly in a dockside pub packed with sailors and watermen. It smelled of tar, tobacco and rum.

"Have a drink," Donnelly said. "You must be feeling weak after all the so-called training your man's giving you." He flashed a smile full of chipped teeth.

"Just a pot of ale," Ebony said.

"Just a pot of ale, eh? Sure you wouldn't prefer a glass of milk?"

"Just a pot of ale."

All round them sailors home from the sea were getting drunk as swiftly as possible, buying drinks for the waterside bawds who often lived with a sailor thoughout his shore leave.

"How's it going?" Donnelly asked.

"Not too bad."

"Not too bad? Last time we met you were sick and tired of it."

"I suppose I still am," Ebony Joe said thoughtfully.

"That's grand," Donnelly said, looking as if he might render a tap-room ballad. "We can double-cross Mr. Blackstone any time you feel like it."

"You mean I can double-cross him."

"Both of us. Does it matter?"

"You killed someone once, didn't you?"

"Who told you that?" Donnelly's choral mood departed. "Blackstone, I suppose. If he's been spreading any lies about me tell him I'll take legal action."

Ebony was bored with Donnelly and his creased punched-in face. "I checked up and it's true."

"What of it? It was a long time ago."

Ebony yawned. "I won't double-cross him. That's what I came to tell you. I'm not going through with it."

"Why have you changed your mind?"

"I never promised I would go through with it."

"You gave me that impression."

"Then it was the wrong impression."

"I've already let it be known you'd cooperate."

"Then you'd better let it be known I won't."

The Irish charm took a crafty turn. "I could probably get some more blunt for you." He tossed back his rum. "How would a hundred pounds suit you?"

It would, Ebony thought, suit me very well. He felt his swollen nose. Blackstone, the bastard. He shook his head. "Forget it," he said.

"I won't forget it," Donnelly said. "Don't you worry, culley. There are ways of making cocky whippersnappers like you cooperate. Sure there are." He moved closer to Ebony.

Ebony pushed him aside and he fell into a group of sailors like a drunk falling into a hammock. They tousled his hair, lifted his wallet and stood him upright.

Donnelly said, "If I were ten years younger . . ."

"You'd still be as useful with your fists as that old trollop over there." Ebony pointed at a rouged, gin-swollen whore in the corner.

"Don't you worry, culley," Donnelly said, face contorted. "you'll come round to *our* way of thinking."

Ebony pushed his way into the night. He thought about the dollymop and decided to postpone his visit. He wasn't sure why. His ear still felt hot and there was a taste of blood in his mouth.

The lights of anchored ships were pulled out across the water in trembling pathways. The shadows shuffled, the air smelled of paint and mud. A ship's siren sounded. The loneliness of the night awoke in Ebony other emotions which he didn't pause to examine. He caught a hackney to Paddington village.

10

Dereliction of duty? Blackstone considered the possibility as he walked past the elegant façades of Bow Street towards the Brown Bear.

Carriages passed spitting mud; a hawker offered him a ballad sheet.

The murderer of Shoemark was still free; the whereabouts of Lily Spender still unknown; his assailant unidentified; the threats still hanging over Cadogan. Worse, in Birnie's view, nothing positive had been done to stop prizefighting.

The old man had been sour. "I'm wondering if I've chosen the wrong man, Blackstone."

Blackstone didn't reply, the eyes of the dead magistrates on the walls accusing him.

"You don't have an interest in prizefighting, do you?" Birnie shuffled through some papers. "You seem to have made more arrests at fights than other Runners."

"I thought Page had made more than me, sir."

"I wasn't including pickpockets.'

Blackstone said, "A prizefight is a natural place to find rogues, sir."

Birnie nodded. "That's why we've got to stop them."

"It seems a pity to close down the hunting grounds."

"There are always the race-courses," Birnie said with distaste.

"I suppose so."

A few months earlier Blackstone had investigated a bookmaker's death. The bookmaker was spotted making a run for it after a favorite had won a race; a mob caught him, tearing off his clothes and his money-pouch and beating him insensible. He died a few days later and a newspaper recorded: "The member of the bookmaking fraternity who so unwisely aroused the ire of the crowds is dead."

"What are you doing about stopping prizefighting?"

"I've spread the word."

"You're usually more positive, Blackstone. Especially if a lodging-house keeper or factory owner is involved."

"Especially if they've been ill-treating children."

"Mmmmm." Justice was Birnie's business, not philanthropy. He pointed his clay pipe like a gun. "I want action."

Blackstone told him about his plan, omitting certain motives. In two day's time there would be a fight and Blackstone intended to break it up. He would demonstrate his zeal, and his failure ten days later to stop Ebony's fight might be excused. He told Birnie he wasn't sure where it was taking place. "It's very difficult. The venue of a fight is never published and details are spread by word of mouth."

Birnie grimaced at the blind beak John Fielding on the wall. He said, "I was a saddlemaker once. I had dealings with the sporting fraternity. Please don't insult my intelligence."

Blackstone turned into the Brown Bear which, in fact, was called The Russian Hotel. It boasted "Lodgings for

124

Gentlemen" and was run by a Mr. G. Hazard, "dealer in foreign wines."

The serving girl was hostile and Blackstone decided that Townshend had described Laura Cadogan to her. He had certainly related Blackstone's reactions to the robberies at the soirée. The other Runners were amused, but bored with Townshend.

"The sooner he retires the better," Ruthven said, a pot of ale hidden in his paw.

"Wellington wouldn't allow it," Page said.

"What's it got to do with him?"

"Townshend's very close to Wellington," said Page, an authority on sycophancy. "He'd have a word in Peel's ear."

Ruthven picked up a copy of the *Morning Herald*. "Talking of Wellington, I see they've chucked out the case you were on in Dublin, Blackie. The riot over Catholic emancipation." He ran a thick finger down the paper. "Placards bearing the slogan, 'Bald-pated Wellesley, you may go home' were exhibited, I see."

"And a bottle or two," Blackstone said. "But the result was a foregone conclusion. No Protestant jury is going to convict a mob rioting against Catholic emancipation."

Saunders, the youngest and newest Runner, overawed by the reputations around him, bought drinks out of turn. He was still excited by his first conviction, a fraud at Reading. A woman told a housewife that she could read the planets, recover stolen goods and get bad debts paid. For every pound she recovered she would take one shilling. She made a fire in the grate and told the victim to put £25 in notes down her bosom. Then she sent the housewife downstairs to fetch some pins and a lock of her husband's hair. She took the notes from her own bosom and put them in a paper parcel with the hair and drew a chalk ring around the chair. With a flourish she threw the pins into the fire and said, "Watch them closely." But the housewife watched the parcel closely and saw the debt-collector substitute another parcel containing plain paper. The woman was sent to a House of Correction for a year.

Saunders would have elaborated on the way he traced the magswoman but the other Runners stopped him.

Ruthven swallowed his ale. "So you're going to stamp out prizefighting, are you, Blackie?"

Blackstone nodded.

"Better you than me."

"I may need your help."

"You'll need more than *my* help."

Page said hopefully, "They'll be looking for you, Blackie. The Fancy, that is. They won't like this," he said with relish. "They won't like it at all."

Saunders said, "If you want any help, Mr. Blackstone . . ."

Blackstone finished his ale, He said, "There's a fight in two days' time. I'm going to stop it."

"You and who else?" Ruthven asked.

"I'm alerting the magistrates—whether they want to be alerted or not. Also the parish constables. And I'm getting authority to call in the Dragoons."

"There's going to be a fight of some sort, then," Ruthven said. "Maybe I'll come along." His fist looked as if it might throttle the tankard.

Blackstone nodded. "A few heads will be broken." He glanced at Page. "Want to come along?" Page said unfortunately he was needed elsewhere, and Blackstone went on, "First I'll officially warn everyone concerned with the fight. Then I'll go into the ring with the magistrates . . ."

"If they turn up," Ruthven said.

Blackstone shrugged. "If the fight starts then the Dragoons charge. At least the Fancy will know I mean business."

"This is the way to really make the Runners unpopular," Ruthven observed.

"Birnie has his reasons," Blackstone said.

"Peel?"

"In a way."

"He's scared of him," Ruthven said. "It makes me sick."

"I don't think he's scared of him. He's doing it for us in a way."

"You're very loyal," Page said.

Ruthven said, "This will put paid to the fight they're all talking about then, eh, Blackie?"

"Which one?" Blackstone asked, knowing.

"The fight between this black lad and the butcher's boy from Bristol."

"Ah, that one," Blackstone said, looking warily at Ruthven.

Ruthven favored him with a battered grin. "But you wouldn't know where that one's held, I suppose."

Blackstone said he didn't.

The girl was waiting at the door as he left. "It sounds like a dangerous job at Wimbledon," she said.

"Eavesdropping again?"

"We can't all be reformers," she said.

The guilt upset him because it was a stranger. When he was younger he had never felt guilty about lifting a watch; or robbing a drunk. Now he had been given trust: his baton, a reproachful, gilt-crowned finger.

He urged the Poacher through Holborn, scattering the indignant crowds.

Perhaps he should cancel the fight. Explain his loyalties to Ebony Joe. But that was another form of betrayal. And for Ebony it would mean back to the Rookery, back to Donnelly, back to years of taking punches: forward to a future as a slow-witted footpad, a bawdy-house bully or a bruiser taking on all-comers at the Queen's Head or the Black Lion.

There was also the old blackbird himself, Ebony's father, fingering the cleanliness of Camden Town as suspiciously as a housemaid's mistress fingers dirt, to be considered.

Blackstone swore at the crowds, thickening as he entered the maze of the Rookery. Jungle eyes watched him from the shadows which the sun had never erased.

In two days he would break up a prizefight, simultaneously taking steps to organize one. Hypocrisy sharpened the guilt. If he could solve the murder, the blackmail, the assault, *something*, the guilt might be assuaged.

He thought about this, reached a decision and guided the Poacher towards the basement where Lawler lived with his thrush.

Which was how Lawler came to be a flashman.

He was affronted at first. Not even a successful flashman. A flashman down on his luck! How low could you get?

He was placated when Blackstone pointed out some of the advantages. Handling the merchandise for instance. And extra expenses. "Call them immoral earnings," Blackstone told him.

All Lawler had to do was tour the bawdy houses,

starting with Kate Hendricks' and working his way down via the Haymarket and the Ratcliffe Highway dance halls to the lodging houses of the docks and the Dials, pretending that he was looking for girls to support him and asking if anyone knew the whereabouts of Lily Spender.

Lawler, already swaggering a little, asked what he should do if any of the resident flashmen attacked him.

"Shoot them," said Blackstone, whose compassion had always eluded Lawler. "Have you got a gun?"

Lawler said he had: a gun was an important tool of his trade when he was unable to pay out on a favorite.

"What if I find the girl?" he asked.

"Stay with her," Blackstone said. "Don't arouse her suspicion. But get word back to me."

"That'll cost more money," Lawler said.

"You're getting paid," Blackstone said, "Don't get greedy, Lawler. Otherwise I might take you round to Bow Street."

Lawler was saddened. "On what charge?"

"Living off fallen women," Blackstone told him.

Dutifully, Lawler began at Kate Hendricks'. He wore flash trimmings to his unremarkable clothes and his voice assumed a bullying tone. There was also about him a new, beefy virility.

At Kate Hendricks' he was a failure. Among the gas-lit swells his chameleon qualities were tested too severely, his polka-dot silks clashing with the white ties and tails. And menacing faces, vicious in the gas-light, materialized when he approached the girls.

Live and let live, Lawler thought.

He moved one step down the scale from Kate's and the other ancestral homes of whoring. And was surprised by his success. Several girls made him financial and physical offers. He was so surprised by their need for security that he wondered if he was in the right profession.

He was particularly taken by a girl named Maisie, a seamstress with punctured fingertips, who supplemented her meagre income by working at night in a bawdy house in Portland Place.

Maisie spent the day sewing shirts. "Four rows of actual stitching, six buttonholes, collars and wristbands. And do you know how much I get for that?" she asked Lawler. "Twopence. But," she added, "I wouldn't mind making one for you for nothing."

Lawler, sensing long-term payment, said he had enough shirts, thinking of the two forlorn garments hanging in his room.

She was about twenty-five and she lived in a single room on the edge of the Devil's Acre slum at Westminster. Lawler guessed she had a child; but she never mentioned it. She was ordinary and under-nourished, with a pale prettiness awaiting encouragement. She didn't fully understand her attraction to gentlemen; but, from what they had said in moments of abandonment, she suspected it was desire for their own dollymops forestalled by their wives.

In the evenings in Portland Place she deflated his new swagger. "You'd never make a flashman," she said.

Lawler was hurt. "Why not? I'm doing all right with you, aren't I?"

"Hardly," Maisie said. "You're paying." And with her customary lack of guile she asked, "Are you married or anything?"

"Only anything," Lawler said.

She laughed. "You're a caution, Lawler." She pulled the sheet over her thin body. "What's your first name?"

Lawler confessed that he hadn't got one; not as far as he knew.

130

"Perhaps Lawler's your first name."

"Perhaps," Lawler said.

"It ought to be Lawless," she said, moving closer to him.

It was only the third night he had been there; but it seemed as if there had been many more; and many more ahead. Lawler saw her making the cocoa while he put out the cat.

She stroked his chest and said, "There isn't much meat on you, is there?" She ran her finger down his ribs. "I could play a tune on them. You need fattening up." (The cat out, the cocoa made.)

"I'd best be going," Lawler said.

"Why? You've paid for longer."

"I've got things to do."

"What, other women?"

Lawler began to dress without answering.

"I shouldn't think you'd be much good to them right now."

Lawler looked at her reprovingly. Coarseness doesn't become a demure seamstress, the look said. But her eyes were moist, and dimly Lawler perceived that the coarseness was armor.

"Will you be back tomorrow?" she asked, as he knotted the silk handkerchief around his neck.

"I don't know, Maisie."

"I'll try and find out about this Lily Spender for you. In fact," she lied, "I might even know where I can find her."

"Then I'll try and come back. But I can't promise anything."

She nodded. "Just try, Lawler. No one can do more than that."

Lawler went to the window. Thin rain was bowling out

131

of the night and the gas-lit street was washed with light. The houses were tall and inviolate. "Funny, isn't it," Lawler said, "you and me in this area without two brass farthings to rub together."

She sat up holding the sheet to her breasts. "The suburbs is where people like you and me belong," she said. "Not the Rookeries, not places like this. Just a little house." She stood beside him. "Surely we're entitled to something, Lawler."

Across the road a manservant put a cat out into the wet night.

11

Blackstone had no difficulty in discovering the venue of the fight. He heard about it in the Daffy Club, the Fives Court, at Tattersalls; behind cupped hands, in dark corners, on scraps of paper.

The site, he was told, was a field in Sussex near Lewes.

The match was between a Jew and a Lancashire navigator renowned for his anti-Semitic feeling. The Jew, called the Touch of Holland's, or the Holland Touch, because his father had been one of the many Jewish immigrants from Amsterdam, was fighting for many things. His race—he was one of the many Jewish boxers who had helped to instill some fear into the Jew-baiting mobs—his own respect, and the purse. His career was almost finished, booze having put him down more times than punches; and by rights he should have been having a benefit at the Fives Court instead of a bare-knuckled milling match. But he had to beat the Jew-hater from Lancashire.

The Lancashireman, Will Bradman, was known as the Hammer because of his ability to smash huge boulders, while digging canals, with a single blow of a hammer. He had great padded shoulders and a mat of body hair that made a collar round his neck. With ale inside him he weighed seventeen stone, but his manager had slimmed him down to fourteen stone for the fight—still thirty pounds heavier than the Jew.

Lancashire boxers had a reputation for dirty fighting: Bradman didn't undermine it. His dirty fighting and his anti-Semitism, combined with the debauched courage of his opponent, real name Aaron Levy, had created considerable interest; although it wasn't championship class and only £100 a side had been put up.

The first threats and attempts against Blackstone's life were made a week before the fight. First, a stone with a piece of paper wrapped round it through his window in Paddington. It said, "Leave milling alone or else."

Two days later, as he rode in Hyde Park, a shot was fired at him from a copse. The ball clattered into the branches of a tree, disturbing the pigeons and making a few horses bolt. Blackstone galloped to the copse but it was empty. The grassland stretching away to Kensington was scattered with horses and any rider could have fired the shot.

He also received more sophisticated threats from Sir Henry Bathurst and Sir Arthur Willoughby at the Pugilistic Club, and from Sir Humphrey Cadogan at White's, the club where General Scott, George Canning's father-in-law, was said to have won £200,000 at whist thanks to his excessive sobriety.

Over boiled fowl and oyster sauce Sir Humphrey, collar sawing a red noose round his neck, asked:

"Have you traced this woman, Lily Spender?"

Blackstone said he hadn't.

"A man's been murdered, I believe."

Blackstone nodded, drinking some champagne.

"So all you have to show for yourself is a dead man?"

"The dead man wrote the letter the girl threatened you with," Blackstone said.

"She's been very quite," Cadogan said. "Perhaps she's frightened. Perhaps she won't carry out her threats."

"How much did you say she wanted?"

"A thousand pounds."

"Then she's ambitious and she'll try again. Although," he added thoughtfully, "it's a lot of money for a girl like that to ask for."

"It's not her," Cadogan said, unwilling to accept such ingratitude. "It's the man. Meyning. He's put her up to it."

"Perhaps. But I can't trace him either."

"I thought you fellows knew everyone in the underworld."

"Not everyone," Blackstone said, mopping up the oyster sauce with a piece of bread.

Cadogan helped himself to a large portion of Stilton and said, "Is there any point in you remaining on this investigation, Blackie?"

"It's up to you. But there has been a murder. I can't abandon that."

Cadogan looked understanding. "I suppose not. But it seems a pity if this girl has decided not to pursue the threats. . . . And don't forget that I'm pretending to be the patron of this black fighter of yours. We wouldn't want that to leak out, would we?" The deviousness of his honest face a good companion to the Stilton. "Especially," he added, "as you're supposed to be putting a stop to prizefighting."

Blackstone waited patiently for the inevitable. It came after the cheese. Leaning confidentially across the table he

135

said, "Surely you don't have to break up this fight between the Jew and the navvy, do you? Let the whole thing rest for a while. I'm sure Birnie will find other things to occupy his Presbyterian mind. And Peel, for that matter."

Blackstone shook his head. "I'm sorry."

"But why, Blackie? You like a spot of milling as much as the next man."

"It's something you wouldn't understand," Blackstone said, not too sure that he understood himself.

"Then you're determined to stop this fight?"

"I am." They moved to the fire for their brandy. "In any case it's not such a wonderful fight. Not exactly an exhibition of pugilistic skill." He looked at Cadogan curiously. "Why are you so concerned about it?"

Cadogan warmed his glass between his hands, sniffing it like a bloodhound. "If you succeed in stopping this fight then you will have proved it can be done. Then you'll have to stop others. Like Ebony Joe versus Billy the Butcher. . . ."

"We'll see," Blackstone said.

"I don't want this fight to be stopped, Blackie. Don't think I'm threatening you," he added, "just warning."

"There's been a lot of warning lately. One way and another. Like your letter."

Cadogan glanced nervously at the other members. "We needn't go into that," he said.

"We needn't," Blackstone agreed. "And I wouldn't want you to think I was threatening you. Just warning."

Sir Humphrey Cadogan, Sir Henry Bathurst and Sir Arthur Willoughby all talked on the assumption that furtive word had reached Blackstone that the fight was to

136

be held near Lewes. Blackstone let the assumption go uncontradicted—and went ahead with his plans to stop the fight on Wimbledon Common, which he knew to be the correct venue.

The Dragoons were quartered three miles away from the site of the fight at a farmhouse with a big yard, encircled by several barns as if the builder had anticipated a siege. The only entrance was barred by a couple of farmhands armed with blunderbusses who explained that cows were calving.

Also present at the farmhouse: Blackstone, three magistrates, a bevy of parish constables and a gang of thugs armed with fairground livetts.

The March day was as gentle as the fight promised to be savage. A daffodil day of budding sunshine and fertility; a tentative day prepared to be snapped shut again by evening frost.

The Fancy streamed along the roads from London as remorselessly, as urgently, as an army in retreat. The roughs and toughs, swells and bloods. In coach, carriage and phaeton, in gigs and carts, on horseback, on foot.

Commerce around Wimbledon had prepared expectantly for the fight. Owners of barns, carts, taverns, stalls, shops. But they were apprehensive because the rowdies trekking down from the north to support Bradman were responding to an unusual discipline. They were seen answering some sort of roll call; and they all carried long cudgels.

Blackstone armed himself with two holster pistols and a couple of his favorite pocket pistol conversions by Perry and Manton. He instructed Lawler to keep an eye on Bagley, the prize-ring commissary, who brought the ring to the site and assembled it. If you followed Bagley you couldn't miss the fight. Aware of this the fancy followed him as if he were the Pied Piper.

From the farmhouse Blackstone went first to the tavern on the common where Aaron Levy was quartered with his manager, seconds and supporters.

Blackstone's arrival with a parish constable and a magistrate (who preferred to wait outside) caused dismay.

Levy was sitting at a table with a jug of claret fortified with brandy. He had been handsome in a swarthy way; but the gypsy features were patched with scar tissue, the skin tough with applications of vinegar. And you could sense slowness of purpose behind the deliberately quick movements. Levy's weapons were courage and an ability to take punishment. Most of the money was on Bradman: most of the southern sympathy was with Levy.

"I'm sorry, Aaron," Blackie said, "you won't be fighting today."

Levy's manager, an old fighter bowed from humping sacks of coal, stood up. "Who says so?"

"I say so." Blackstone pointed his baton at the manager's stomach, his other hand on the butt of a pistol.

"Why do you want to spoil everyone's fun?" Levy asked, pouring himself claret.

"I don't want to. You're breaking law, that's all. It's my job to enforce it."

The other members of the Holland Touch's party edged closer.

The parish constable, middle-aged and respected, took up a discreet position behind Blackstone.

Blackstone said, "I have to inform you that if any attempt is made to hold this match I shall have no alternative but to arrest you."

"And Bradman?" Levy asked.

"Both of you."

"His supporters will like that," Levy said. "They've come a long way to see him get beat by me. Some of them have been on the road for two days."

Blackstone shrugged. In the background he noticed one of the seconds leaving the tavern.

The manager tried another tactic. He tried to put his arm round Blackstone, saying, "You look like a sporting gentleman, Mr. Blackstone. Such a shame spoiling the fun for everyone." He gestured across the common. "We all know it's against the law. But it always has been and no one's taken no notice. Why, some of the real gentry have come down to see Aaron here make mincemeat of the Hammer." He looked around the parlor but all the real gentry had left when Blackstone walked in.

Blackstone gave him a small prod with his baton. "There won't be any fight," he said.

The manager spat on the floor. "A pox on you," he said.

Levy stood up, fingering the single ear-ring (which he always removed before a fight since an opponent had ripped one away, taking the lobe of his left ear with it). "You'll regret this, my culley," he said.

"Threatening me, Levy?"

"Stating a fact."

"Then I'll state a fact, Levy. If you try and take part in this fight I'll personally arrange your training—on the treadmill."

A man swore at the back of the crowd and a bottle sailed through the air, missing Blackstone's head and exploding against the wall.

Blackstone thrust his way through the throng and

139

found the bottle-thrower, isolated by his friends. He hit him in the stomach and then on the jaw. "Anybody else?"

Levy stared at him, panting as if he'd been hit. "You'd like to fight me, wouldn't you? Give me a little exertion before the milling so that Bradman would have a better chance. Then put your money on him, eh? Never short of a bit of blunt, you Runners, are you?"

"As a matter of fact, my culley," Blackstone said. "If I were a betting man I'd put my blunt on you." He walked to the door. "*If* I were a betting man." He massaged his knuckles. "Don't make me stop the fight, Levy. I don't want to see you on the cockchafer."

He mounted the Poacher and rode to the inn where Bradman and his mob were quartered. Something was wrong: he could feel it. Something in the attitude of Levy's supporters, a muted confidence beneath the outrage. But why worry with the Dragoons standing by?

He passed a glade surrounded by a silver birch where there was a small fair. An Italian organ-grinder, a strong man in a leopard skin, a peepshow, a small German band competing with the organ-grinder, a menagerie including a docile wildcat which looked as if its "savage domane" was a fireside rug, a freak called the "Living Skeleton" devouring a steak, some gypsy fortune-tellers, a couple of drinking booths, a thimble rigger and a card-sharp and a shy with an arsenal of livetts.

Somewhere above, a skylark perched on the sunshine and sang rapturously.

The tavern seemed strangely silent. A thatched, mellow place with a chain across the parlor separating the swells from the commoners.

When Blackstone pushed open the door he saw the fire, pale in the sunshine. A jovial host, two or three drinkers.

140

Some possessions on the tables—bookmakers' pouches, canes, hats—indicating that there were more customers than he could see.

It was his last conscious thought for a while.

The cudgel hit him on the back of the neck, the blow softened by the thick satin on the collar of his new spring coat.

When he came to he was in a cellar surrounded by barrels of ale and wine. Above, a grating pierced by a shaft of sunlight. He could hear voices outside, the drone of a hurdy-gurdy, and the faraway sound of cheering.

He struggled to get free but his feet and hands were bound with window cord; he was also gagged with a cloth. He felt sick and cold and his head ached.

He lay still for a few moments. Twice, now, he had been knocked out. Anger began to counter the coldness. The humiliation his punishment for duplicity? If the fight took place the humiliation was complete.

Why hadn't they killed him? he wondered. Presumably because his assailants were content if this one fight took place: their money was laid and the future of prizefighting could take care of itself. Also they wouldn't want the blood of a Bow Street officer on their hands.

The footsteps were hesitant but distinct. Floorboards creaking, a chair scraping.

Blackstone lay still.

Above him a door opened. The daylight under the cellar door became brighter. Someone was coming down the stairs.

Blackstone's topcoat was open, spread under him. Both pistols gone.

The footsteps stopped on the other side of the door.

The door inched open as if a baby were pushing it.

"Hallo, Mr. Blackstone," said Lawler. "What are you doing down here?"

"The fight's started," Lawler told him as they drank brandy in the parlor—Blackstone to revive himself, Lawler to keep him company.

"How long's it been on?"

"It's only just started."

"How the hell did you find me here?" Blackstone felt the tenderness at the back of his neck.

"It wasn't so difficult," Lawler said with pride, awaiting the gratitude. "I knew you had to visit both taverns. I went first to the Holland Touch's but they said you'd been and gone. So I came here."

Blackstone said, "One of Levy's seconds came over here and warned them."

"Didn't you think of that?" Lawler asked.

Blackstone shook his head and winced. "Does it look like it?" He drank some more brandy. "Why's the fight started? Surely I wasn't the only person who could stop it? We've got magistrates, parish constables, God knows how many Dragoons. And a few villains on our side." He looked pointedly at Lawler. "If villains are ever on our side."

"They are if they're paid enough," Lawler said, thinking that it was time for gratitude.

"You'll get what's due to you," Blackstone said. "Now tell me why the fight hasn't been stopped."

"Several reasons," Lawler said.

"Which are?" Blackstone poured himself more brandy, leaving Lawler's glass empty.

"In the first place no one's as keen to get the milling

stopped as you. And as you know the magistrates are scared stiff."

"Go on. What about the Dragoons?"

"They're still up at the farm I shouldn't wonder."

"What are they doing—dressage?"

Lawler helped himself to brandy. "I don't know about that, Mr. Blackstone. The point is"—he looked at Blackstone apprehensively—"the point is you were also outwitted about the place where the fight's taking place. They thought you might not fall for Lewes so they picked a third site about two miles away from here. Most of the Fancy knew about it," Lawler added.

"And how do you know about it, Lawler?"

"Because I did what you told me to—I followed Bagley. He began to put up the ring. But sort of furtively, like he was a stickman waiting for the swag to be slipped to him. I hung around and saw several of Bradman's men—and Levy's, too—walking around delivering some sort of message. I also noticed a lot of them moving away. You got me, Mr. Blackstone?"

"I've got you, Lawler."

"Then Bagley packed up his gear and moved off as well. I followed him. About two miles away he started putting up the ring in earnest. Struth," Lawler said, "what a performance. Bradman's men made a sort of enclosure outside the outer ring. Charging anything up to five shillings they was. And if anyone argued they cracked their heads open with their sticks."

"How many rounds has the fight been going?"

Lawler shrugged. "Not all that many. I left when it started. To come and find you," he added, reproachfully. "I borrowed a horse. . . . I suppose it's been on about half an hour. It could be a long 'un. They reckon Holland

143

Touch'll lose all right, but he'll take a lot of knock-downers before he packs it in. Otherwise he won't get much of a collection."

"Is the Poacher still outside?"

Lawler nodded.

"Have you got a gun?"

Lawler said he had and Blackstone said, "Give it to me."

"Do you think I did well, Mr. Blackstone?"

Blackstone buttoned his dusty coat. "You'd have done better if you'd alerted the Dragoons instead of looking for me."

"I wish I had," Lawler said as Blackstone climbed on to the Poacher and galloped off to the farm.

The Dragoons were lined up behind a wood, blue and grey uniforms hardly visible against the sky. To their left, a pond filled with blue light from the sky; to their right the green arena of the fight. High above the ring where the two bloodied men fought the skylark still sang.

Blackstone reined in the Poacher on the outskirts of the crowd. No one took much notice. Bradman's bullies, having sold their "enclosure," had now invaded the inner ring reserved for umpires, referees, patrons and privileged, titled or even Royal swells.

The fighters were still handing out sharp, cutting blows, aimed at giving the Fancy enough blood and bruises for their money; avoiding the heavy clouts that could break their knuckles or dislocate their forearms.

Bradman was using his usual tactics: throwing Levy and falling on him hoping to split his ribs, stepping on his foot, pulling his hair (a play which had been used by Gentleman John Jackson) and getting his head in chancery while he pummelled it with his fist.

But Levy had an answer. Because it was a foul to hit a man who had one hand and one knee on the ground, Levy made darting attacks and, before Bradman had time to counter, dropped to one knee with one hand touching the ground.

The tactic upset the Hammer's supporters and they appealed to the referee. But during a flurry of blows it was difficult to see if Levy had gone down deliberately. The referee indicated this. One cudgel got him on the shoulder and a stone hit him on the head.

The guardians of the outer ring tried to clear it; but they were too old for Bradman's disciplined young mob.

Blackstone leaned down from the Poacher and tapped a farmer on the shoulder. "How's it going?"

The farmer looked up but showed no recognition. "Not bad. A lot of fibbing to come yet before the Hammer finally puts paid to Levy." His vowels as juicy as cider apples.

"What round?"

"Twenty-three by my reckoning. I reckon it'll go another fifty."

"I doubt if it will last another one," Blackstone said.

Blackstone checked the two holster guns and Lawler's pocket pistol. Down in the green bowl Levy had fallen, Bradman on top of him; blood was oozing from the Jew's mouth.

"Hey," said the farmer, "I hope you're not right." He looked relieved as Levy got to his feet. "No, it'll go another fifty. In his day Levy could have flattened Bradman. Trouble is he got pickled inside and out." The farmer's laugh faded as Blackstone nosed the Poacher through the crowd, a long-barreled pistol in one hand.

The Fancy parted indignantly.

Half-way to the ring Blackstone spotted a magistrate

and called out to him. The magistrate answered half-heartedly, trying to edge away. Blackstone went after him. "Magisterial authority," he said, "is what we need. You'd better follow me."

"You're asking for trouble," the magistrate said. "They'll kill you."

"Not with you present," Blackstone said. Experimentally, he pointed the pistol at the magistrate's head. "We must have the full majesty of the law present."

The magistrate followed him.

When he was close to the outer ring Blackstone spotted some of his own paid thugs armed with livetts waiting behind Bradman's bullies.

"And where were you?" he shouted.

"Waiting for you, Blackie," they replied.

Blackstone took their point. "You needn't wait much longer." He grinned as they waved their livetts.

In front of him referee, umpires, seconds, fighters waited. He tied the Poacher to a rope and addressed himself to Bradman's corner. "Good afternoon, gentlemen. Is this the first time we've met today?"

Bradman's manager, a former milkman, said, "What the hell are you doing here spoiling everyone's enjoyment?" He sought the support of the spectators. "Why don't you go and find some thieves?"

"Because most of them are here," Blackstone said.

The Hammer spoke. "Just let me finish off the Jew. Then I'll call it a day."

"Was it you who hit me?" Blackstone said.

The manager stuck a towel over Bradman's mouth as he began to speak.

In the other corner Levy watched and waited.

Blackstone glanced towards the trees where the Dragoons were hidden.

146

He dismounted and climbed into the ring, pulling the plump and respected magistrate behind him.

He held up his baton. "You all know what this is?" A murmur of recognition. Blackstone shouted, "Then I'm afraid I've got bad news for you. This fight has got to stop. It's not my decision—it's the decision of your Government."

A voice suggested a fate for the Government. A livett flayed. Slurry, snarling voices and a scream of pain.

The skylark stopped singing and flew south.

"I'm sorry I've got to spoil your sport."

The Fancy were sorry, too. A clod of turf catapulted into the ring. The referee departed, followed by the magistrate. Bradman's supporters flourished their cudgels.

Blackstone tried for the last time, hand held high, pistol catching slivers of sunlight. "The fight must stop. That's the law."

"You're a brave man, my culley," someone shouted. "And a dead one."

The spectators bawled their agreement.

Blackstone fired the pistol.

The explosion rippled across the warm pool of the afternoon. Then a moment's silence.

One voice was joined by a thousand others, "It's the Dragoons."

The horses were trotting with ceremonial decorum. In front, a young officer, with a sad and handsome face beneath his plumes.

The crowd stayed still, the participants in the inner ring frozen in a tableau.

At the brink of the green bowl the horses broke into a gallop. The crowd scattered.

Someone shouted, "Get the Runner. Get the bastard."

Bradman seized a cudgel and came at Blackstone.

147

Blackstone dodged the slow swing of the club and hit the fighter's battered, pickled features with his fist; but Bradman's face was used to blows like that. He shook his head and grinned. "I don't need this," he said, throwing down the cudgel.

Blackstone remembered what he had taught Ebony; skill, speed, agility. He feinted with his left and hit the Lancashireman good and low with his right.

He heard a shout, "Get the bastard's horse."

He saw two men going for the Poacher with cudgels. The Poacher reared up, pawing at them with his front hooves.

The Dragoons were four hundred yards away, sabres slashing the air.

Bradman grunted from the blow, hands to his groin.

Blackstone grabbed the cudgel and cracked it over his skull. Bradman pitched forward, blood dripping from the wound on to the thick mats covering his body.

Blackstone saw one man with a cudgel aiming at the Poacher's hind legs. Blackstone found Lawler's pistol in his pocket and fired through the cloth. The ball hit the man in the thigh.

The frantic crowds were streaming away, a rabble army in retreat; Waterloo at Wimbledon.

Blackstone mounted the Poacher as the Dragoons galloped past, ignoring the fight raging between Bradman's bullies and Blackstone's thugs armed with fairground livetts.

The cudgels were heavy and lethal, but unwieldy; the livetts lighter and more manageable, but lacking the scything power of the cudgels. Crossbow versus longbow. Half a dozen bodies lay on the grass.

The Dragoons reached the fleeing Fancy, slashing with the flats of their sabres. One or two blades landed at an unfortunate angle, drawing blood and exposing bone. The sad face of the handsome young officer had brightened.

The Dragoons took the small fair in style, rattling the Living Skeleton's ribs with a sabre, debilitating the strong man with a hoof, rampaging through the drinking booth, changing the fireside wildcat into a spitting fury.

But it was all over really.

The officer reined in his grey charger and saluted Blackstone; the ironic sort of salute the military reserves for civilians. Blackstone raised his baton.

"Everything to your satisfaction?" the officer asked.

Blackstone said it was.

"Field planning went a bit astray, I understand."

"There was a misunderstanding."

"These things happen," the officer said. *In civilian life but not in the Dragoons.*

Blackstone's head was throbbing. "Nevertheless," he said pointing at the Living Skeleton strumming his bruised ribs, "a great victory."

The officer looked at him doubtfully and rode off.

Blackstone rode back across the battlefield to the ring. Livett had beaten cudgel and the victors were pillaging the vanquished. They stopped when Blackstone arrived.

Aaron Levy, the Touch of Holland's, was still in the ring.

Blackstone waved at him. "I did your job for you, Levy."

"You and the Dragoons," Levy said. He climbed out of the ring and put on his coat. "I had the bastard beat," he said.

149

"With another fifty rounds to go?"

"Who said there were another fifty?"

"The Fancy likes its money's worth."

"It was my last chance," Levy said. Slowly, he walked away towards the bruised and hopeless future.

A couple of magistrates and a parish constable returned importantly to the scene. The magistrate Blackstone had led to the ring said, "Good work, Blackstone. I want to congratulate you . . ."

But Blackstone was galloping away across the trampled grass.

The saffron afternoon deepened to gold and the skylark returned from the south.

"To think," Laura Cadogan said, bathing the wound at the back of his neck, "that I once distrusted you."

"How could you?" Blackstone asked. He was sitting on the bed in the house in Hanover Square.

She was dressed only in a chemise to avoid staining any celestial blue with soap and water.

"I'm very proud of you."

"It's one way of getting reforms done."

"It's not the only way." He felt her breasts pushing at his back. "We're hoping to get a bill through Parliament."

"There's already been one. Prizefighting's illegal."

"We're making the law stronger."

"Are you indeed?"

She dried the wound with a towel. "There, now you must get some sleep."

"I must," he said turning and slipping the chemise down over her shoulders.

She shivered. "I never thought I'd like this . . ."

". . . sort of thing?"

She nodded. "I never though I'd like men."

"Couldn't you keep that in the singular?"

She said she could; breathlessly as his hands touched her breasts.

Then he kissed the scar because that was the way they always began these days.

12

Ebony Joe's father was kidnapped five days before the fight with Houseman.

He was trying to make his room in Camden Town look more lived-in when the three men knocked at the door. Standing the sentinel volumes in the bookcase at ease, distributing soot in the fireplace, rumpling the bed; although the room still looked unnaturally clean.

He opened the door, stumbling as the men pushed past him. He pulled a gummy face and one of them slapped him, not realizing that it was his only expression.

They looked like bruisers, wearing shabby velveteen coats, breeches and half-boots, with handkerchiefs masking their faces.

The spokesman said, "You're coming with us."

The old man tried to alter his expression but the plea and the thanks of the beggar were deep and permanent. He asked, "Where are we going?"

They slapped him again and knocked him across the bed.

One of the bruisers said, "Don't be too hard on him. We don't want him to snuff it."

They bound his arms behind his back and gagged him, which was unnecessary because a cry for help after dark attracted little attention.

They took him away in a cart pulled by a moth-eaten horse, dumped him in a cellar near the river, took off his gag and bonds and gave him some gruel. "Because we don't want you to snuff it," the spokesman repeated.

"Why?" asked the old man, drinking the gruel in his practical way.

The third said, "None of your business, me old blackbird."

They left him in the rustling gloom, locking the door behind them.

At least, thought Ebony Joe's father peering around, it seemed to be dirty.

Ebony Joe read aloud, with difficulty, the account of the Dragoons' charge in *Bell's Life in London*. It was by the Pierce Egan who was reputed to have written the book *Boxiana: or Sketches of Ancient and Modern Pugilism, from the days of the Renowned Broughton and Slack to the Heroes of the Present Milling Era*, dedicated in 1812 to Captain Barclay. Egan had also collaborated with Cruikshank in producing the panoramic *A Picture of the Fancy on the road to Moulsey Hurst*.

"You certainly aren't the most popular man in London, Mr. Blackstone," Ebony said.

Blackstone shuffled the other journals. *Bell's Life in London, The Weekly Dispatch, The Morning Post, The Times*. . . .

"Somebody loves me."

"Who?" Ebony demanded.

They were sitting in Blackstone's kitchen eating steaks after the morning training session.

Blackstone picked up *The Times*. "They do," he said. "Heroic is the word they use."

Ebony belched. "They're the only ones." He paused. "Why did you do it, Mr. Blackstone?"

"Because I had to."

"And what about my fight—are you going to stop that?" He chewed thoughtfully. "Because if you are I can't see much point in all this chasing about every perishing morning."

Blackstone leaned back in his chair, adjusting his dressing-gown. The girl from the Brown Bear sat sulkily in front of the fire, making tea from the kettle on the hob.

He said, "No, I shan't be stopping your fight, Ebony."

"What are you going to do then?"

"I'm not quite sure. But I have an idea." He turned to the girl. "Perhaps you could go and clean up the other room."

"Clean it yourself."

Blackstone kissed the nape of her neck. "Please."

"Would the Honorable Miss Laura Cadogan clean it for you?"

Thinking that he wouldn't even ask her, Blackstone said, "I'm sure she wouldn't, the bitch."

"Give me another kiss, then."

Blackstone gave her another and closed the door behind her.

He looked speculatively at Ebony, who was trying to mop the pattern off his plate with a chunk of bread. "What I'm going to say is between the two of us. Understood?"

"Understood," Ebony replied in a bread-muffled voice.

"It's in your interests. If this fight gets stopped then you're finished because you'll be bad luck. You know how superstitious the Fancy is." He paused, doubtfully—but

155

Ebony would have to know sooner or later. "You see," he explained, "everyone thinks now that I'm determined to stop prizefighting."

"Aren't you?"

Blackstone said, "So it will be just like the Hammer's fight. The Fancy will try and lead me to the wrong venue again. Because, of course, they don't know I'm your patron. Anyway," Blackstone hurried through the deception, "I'll arrive at the wrong place even though I know the right one. You see," he added, "the law will trust my judgment after my last success . . ."

"Won't you be there to see the fight then?"

"I'll see what can be done."

"Strike me," Ebony said. "You're taking a risk, aren't you?"

"I am," Blackstone said. "I only hope it's worth it."

That night Ebony paid his twice-weekly visit to his father in Camden Town.

The note was weighted to the table by a piece of coal. Ebony read it laboriously, then sat down in front of the dead fire, fists tightly clenched.

A lot of money was still being laid on Houseman. Blackstone worried about it as he rode along the edge of the Holy Land, the St. Giles Rookery, where criminals operating in adjacent rich pastures found asylum among the choked alleys and suffocated passages.

Blackstone, elegant in new spring clothes this March morning, mounted on the equally well-groomed Poacher, stared into the labyrinths of his birthplace. A row of tenements under which cellars were joined to form an escape route; a tavern roof forming a stepping-stone on

156

another well-trodden pathway. Beside the tavern stood a worm-eaten cottage where Blackstone had caught a gang of coiners; at the end of a corkscrew lane a brothel with underground passages leading to the West End; behind it a sorting-house of squalor called Jones Court, guarded by a bull-terrier.

Whenever Blackstone went to the Holy Land he thought of Henry Challoner. Each had emerged from the slum, taking different routes: Challoner to the highest echelon of crime, Blackstone to the highest echelon of crime prevention. Looking at the derelict humanity—thieving and fighting to escape starvation—which he was supposed to control, Blackstone wondered who had been right.

A one-eyed pieman waved at Blackstone. "Never learn, will you, Blackie?"

Blackstone reined in the Poacher, dismounted and gave him twopence. The pieman thrust a baked hand into his small oven and gave him a crusty pie, drooling with gravy.

The pieman said, "One of these days the people of the Rookery will get you, Blackie. They never forget."

Blackstone munched and shrugged. He said, "The Runners are quite popular. Almost as popular as highwaymen."

"Not round here they aren't. Leastways you're not, my culley. A nose is never popular, is he, Blackie? You know that." His socket reproached Blackstone.

"I leave them alone as much as I can." Blackstone's voice hardened. "But not your lodging-house keepers, not your skinners, not your kidsmen."

The pieman said, "Them as lives in the Holy Land don't know about such niceties. My advice to you is to stay well away. If there's anywhere left for you to go," he added.

"What do you mean?"

"Seems you're very matey with the Dragoons these days."

Blackstone wiped his fingers with a silk handkerchief.

"Nice wipe you've got there," the pieman said. "I should hang on to it." He pointed at a group of boys eyeing the handkerchief speculatively.

Blackstone said, "Are you a betting man?"

"I'm not a member of the Fancy, if that's what you mean. A one-eyed pieman wouldn't stand much chance with some of the villains on the road to Moulsey." He served one of the boys with a baked potato which the boy shared with two others. "But I have a bet now and again."

"Who do you fancy in this mill between Ebony Joe and Billy the Butcher?"

"Funny you should mention that," the pieman said. "I was only talking about it this morning. Everyone reckons the black kid. And yet there's a mint of money going on the Bristol boy. Mind you," he said, "I don't see much point in laying a wager on either if you're going to break it up."

"Why do you reckon the money's going on Houseman?"

The pieman dodged a plume of sparks from the oven. "I don't know, Blackie. Your guess is as good as mine." Single shrewd eye peering at Blackstone. "But it's beginning to look as if there might be a cross, isn't it?"

"It's beginning to look that way."

"Which can only mean that Ebony Joe has been persuaded not to give of his best."

"Nonsense," Blackstone snapped.

"How would you know, Blackie?"

Blackstone didn't reply.

158

The pieman said, "It stands to reason, doesn't it? Some cove's got at the sambo."

"The Fancy wouldn't stand for it," Blackstone said.

"They've stood for it before and they'll stand for it again. The times I've heard that a fight's been crossed. But it's never stopped anyone going to see it. And there's always the chance that someone's had a word in the ear of the other fighter as well. So we get two crooked fighters coming up to the scratch. Which makes it much the same as if they was both straight, doesn't it, Blackie? In any case there's always a chance that if one fighter's taken some blunt to throw the fight he'll think again and give as good as he gets. No, Blackie"—the pieman shook his head with conviction—"the smell of a cross never had much effect on the Fancy."

"I suppose you're right," Blackstone said.

The pieman said, "Now, if you could find out the cove who's putting most of the brass on the Bristol boy, that might be interesting."

The blind socket seemed to be full of sly intuition.

The pieman went on, "But you can't be all that interested, can you, Blackie?" He warmed his hands on a potato. "Why should you be? If you're out to stop the milling, that is."

"I'm trying to stop it," Blackstone said. "But the Fancy will be a bit more clever this time." He wrapped some silver coins in the silk handkerchief and tied it in a knot.

"What's the betting on the match?" the pieman asked.

"Evens," Blackstone told him. "It ought to be four to six on Ebony Joe."

"You seem to have taken a shine to that boy, Blackie. Anything to do with your name?"

159

"Perhaps," Blackstone said. "Anyway, keep your ears open."

"For what, Blackie?"

"For the source of the money going on Houseman." He gave the pieman a sovereign.

The pieman saluted, winking with his good eye.

Blackstone whistled over one of the boys eating the potato. "Here," he said, "share this between you." He tossed the boy the silken purse.

Then he mounted the Poacher and rode to Bow Street, nursing his worry.

Birnie was in a coffee house near the courthouse. He was alone at a table, sipping a steaming mug of coffee and blowing thin jets of pipe-smoke towards the other customers.

"You're taking a bit of a risk," Blackstone said, sitting down. "Coming to places like this."

"I've got my Runners to protect me," Birnie said.

But he looked vulnerable sitting there, Blackstone thought. The beak who daily dispatched much of the coffee house's clientele to Newgate, the hulks, Botany Bay, the gallows. Armed only with the majesty of the law—not so majestic when you're staring down the barrel of a blunderbuss.

Birnie said, "I hope I can look forward to a repeat of your success at Wimbledon."

Blackstone gulped his coffee.

"Well?"

"I hope so too, sir."

"Have you made any plans?"

"I'm making them."

"Could you be more specific?"

"The same sort of thing. As soon as I get to know the venue I'll get you to call in the military."

"Mmmmm." Birnie stroked his thin face—shrewdness becoming suspicion in the eyes of the guilty. "Won't they be a bit more clever this time?"

"Perhaps," Blackstone said. "But I have my informants."

"I hope so, Blackstone." Birnie paused. "The black boy's fight is only a supporting bout, isn't it?"

Blackstone said it was.

"Then can you tell me why it's attracted so much interest?"

"There's a lot of money being wagered," Blackstone told him.

"So I gather. Is it a cross?" The cant sounded incongruous from Birnie. He added, "Don't look surprised. I'm a magistrate, not a clergyman." He waited. "Well, is it?"

"It could be, I suppose."

"But, of course, you don't know too much about these things."

"I know enough, sir. After all, you can't be in our business without knowing a bit about the Fancy."

"That's true," Birnie said, staring at Blackstone. "Nor can you be a magistrate without knowing a bit about its members." He aimed his pipe at Blackstone. "Anything on the Shoemark murder?"

"Nothing, sir."

"Or the blackmail?"

Blackstone shook his head and said, "At least I broke up the Wimbledon fight."

"Yes," Birnie said, "at least you did that." He stood up. "I've left my purse in the office. Please attend to the bill."

"Very well, sir."

Blackstone nodded absently as Birnie walked out, leaving behind a wake of hatred. He had forgotten that Ebony's fight was a supporting bout: suddenly it seemed to have a new significance.

Later that day Blackstone made several moves.

He went to Lawler's basement in the Rookery and dispatched him in search of the bookmaker who had taken the first £5,000 bet on Houseman.

Then he went to various citadels of the Fancy where he was received with hostility. He refused drinks in case they were poisoned and listened politely while they fed him the wrong venue and the wrong date.

And he visited the house of reform where Laura Cadogan worked to make sure that she wasn't going to her father's mansion within the next few days.

It was a brown, wooden building leaning over the road with the weight of its goodness. Although the ragged clerks bowed over tracts didn't seem to have benefited much from reform.

Blackstone talked to Laura in her office. As he went in two of her colleagues left hastily. Blackstone asked if she had parted with much money to finance their work. She kissed him and said she hadn't.

He left reluctantly, feeling a great need for her; especially seeing her in her prim clothes and knowing what lay beneath.

Before leaving for Cadogan's mansion, where he planned to finish Ebony's training, he returned to Bow Street.

There he learned that Meyning had been arrested in Southwark and charged at Union Street with the murder of Lily Spender.

He rode to Southwark and questioned the officers and Meyning who had signed a confession.

Meyning had throttled the girl and given her body to some tinkers to dispose of. But they had become scared and dumped it in a warehouse on the riverside.

The aspect of the crime which intrigued Blackstone was the fact that Lily Spender had died before the date on the letter threatening Sir Humphrey Cadogan.

13

Blackstone poured himself a glass of Cadogan's port and stared at the pale sunset. There had been a storm and the last of the crocuses were flattened around the boles of the trees, as if each had been squashed with a fist. Light rain tapped on the window; a dog trotted importantly through the daffodils.

He rolled the port around in his mouth. He was now sure of one thing: everything was connected. By gossamer threads, perhaps, but connected. Blackmail, murder, Ebony's fight. His own betrayal of Birnie.

He poured himself more port.

A maid knocked timorously on the door and asked if everything was all right. "For the moment," Blackstone said, smiling at her. She curtsied and retreated to the depths where she knew she belonged.

The sun went down, leaving behind greyish light. A wind gathered force, clattering the budding branches, pressing the rain against the windows.

Before returning to London he had to interview Cadogan's two fallen women. But first he had to see Cadogan himself.

The sky darkened, rain sprayed against the windows. The lights from the quarters of the well-paid servants made a shining pathway across the cobbled courtyard.

Cadogan's complexion was even rosier than usual; his manner hearty, as if his troubles had been solved. He wasn't pleased to see Blackstone, but Blackstone was accustomed to this reaction. He was dressed in hunting pink.

"Hallo, Blackie," he said. "Good to see you." The tone belying the words. "I see you've helped yourself to the port." He poured himself a glassful, drank it in one gulp and poured himself another.

"I gather," Blackstone said, "that you caught the fox."

Sir Humphrey nodded, taking up his position separating visitors from the fire.

Blackstone said, "You seem to be in a very relaxed mood. Rather different from the last time we met here."

Sir Humphrey did a small knees-bend in front of the blazing logs and said, "Things are a bit different now, Blackie. No more threats from that girl."

"It's hardly surprising." Blackstone watched him carefully.

"Why's that, Blackie?"

"Because she's dead," Blackstone said.

"Ah." The color didn't leave his cheeks; but the strength left his legs. "Ah." He sat down in the deep leather armchair. "Dead, did you say?"

"Dead," Blackstone told him. "Murdered."

"Ah."

The rain spattered against the window and the branches talked.

166

"She was killed by Meyning," Blackstone told him. "They had a quarrel. He wanted her back on the streets and she refused. He's made a full confession."

"Poor girl," Cadogan said. He poured himself more port. "If she'd taken my advice and gone into service she would have been alive today. Despite what she did to me I feel sad for her."

"What did she do?"

"You know what she did—threatened me."

Blackstone took some snuff, thoughtfully turning the warm gold box in his hand. "I know she threatened you orally," he said. "At least, according to you she did."

Cadogan stood up and turned his buttocks to the fire. "What the devil are you talking about? She threatened me orally *and* by letter."

"She writes a very good letter for a dead woman," Blackstone said.

Cadogan said, "For God's sake stop talking in riddles."

"She was dead before the date on that letter."

"Then she must have dictated it before she died."

"Then why would she have post-dated it?"

"Perhaps the letter-writer made a mistake."

"No," Blackstone said, "I don't think he did. Shoemark wasn't the sort to make professional mistakes."

They considered the implications. Tiny flames leaped in their glasses; rain tapped on the windows—reminding Blackstone of prisoners tapping messages on walls.

After a while Cadogan said, "Well at least it's an end to the blackmailing. If it was Meyning doing it and not the girl."

"Perhaps," Blackstone said.

"What do you mean, perhaps? One dead and one in jail—a difficult partnership for blackmail, Blackie." A smile

167

touched his aristocratic features. "It rather looks," he continued, "as if I shan't be needing your services any longer."

The maid returned, looking at her master nervously. "One of the ladies across the way wants to see you, sir."

Cadogan pulled at his lower lip. "Tell her I'll see her in half an hour."

When the maid had gone Cadogan said, "At least these two poor girls are grateful. . . ."

"Any replacements on their way?" Blackstone asked.

"As a matter of fact there are. Two poor girls from respectable homes who were forced to sell themselves in the Haymarket."

"So you're chucking these two out?"

"I'm handing them over to someone who will get them into service."

Blackstone looked at his watch, thinking about the next job without pleasure, and said, "You seem to be forgetting one thing."

Cadogan's fingers sought the noose of chafed flesh at his neck. "What's that, Blackie?"

"The letter you wrote. The love letter," he said, hauling down aristocracy to a penny novelette.

"Surely Meyning's got that."

"I don't think so. I questioned him closely. He didn't know anything about a letter. And I don't think he knew anything about any blackmail."

"And you believed a man like that?" Cadogan asked uncertainly. "A pimp, a murderer?"

"I'm afraid so. He had no reason to lie."

"Then it was Lily Spender on her own."

"If you believe a dead woman can write threatening letters."

"It's all very disturbing." Cadogan combed his grey hair with his fingers.

168

Blackstone pursued him. "Don't forget that a man has been murdered because of your behavior. And don't forget that someone has still got that letter of yours."

"Well, whoever's got it hasn't done anything with it."

"Not yet," Blackstone said. "They're probably getting it copied for circulation to all the societies and clubs you belong to. In particular to the society examining the plight of fallen women. I believe," he added, "that they're preparing a report for Parliament."

Cadogan sank back into the chair.

"Never mind," Blackstone said, "you caught that old fox today."

In the corridor outside he met Amy Lawson, the outgoing whore.

He said, "Hallo, Amy. Going in for your daily lecture on now to be a good girl?"

"The old bastard's chucking us out," Amy Lawson said.

"You don't sound very grateful for what he's done for you."

"It's not the first time I've had that done," Amy said.

"And you're going into service?"

"Into service? Into harness." She shook her head. "Not likely, culley. You won't catch me in cap and gown emptying the master's chamber pot."

"Back to the old game then?"

She nodded and Blackstone glimpsed despair behind the rouge.

"If you're ever in trouble you know where to come."

She took hold of his arm. "Can I see you before I go, Blackie?"

"How much?"

"Not a touch. I've got something to tell you. Something that may help you. Although God knows why I should want to help you."

"All right," Blackstone said. "I'll come round to your room tonight."

She gave him a wink. "You won't be disappointed."

Blackstone grinned. "Nor will you," he said.

Ebony arrived by mail coach with the dented tin box in which he kept all his possessions. A lot of the cheek had left him.

They left the box in his room and went to the gymnasium where two or three fighters were lounging around awaiting the miraculous onset of fitness. Donnelly was in London.

"Anything to tell me, Ebony?" Blackstone said.

Ebony, stripped to his running gear, shook his head. A handsome head, Blackstone thought, not intended for systematic destruction. Ebony said, "Except that I don't see any point in running.

"Why?"

Ebony shrugged, muscles primed, no spare fat beneath the sleek black skin. "I'm fit enough."

"That's the only reason?"

"Of course it's the only reason." He began jogging, face turned away from Blackstone.

"Off you go then. Two miles or so will do."

It was getting dark, with a breeze undecided between spring and winter coming over the fields.

"Aren't you coming with me?"

Blackstone said he wasn't; Ebony looked relieved rather than outraged.

Blackstone watched him down the road; elbows tucked into his ribs, supporting his loneliness on hunched shoulders.

Then he took the key of the tin box from Ebony's coat,

170

went to his room and opened the box. Disgusted with himself.

At the bottom he found a leather wallet—tooled, probably, from a coat-tail pocket at a prizefight—and rifled the contents. He found what he was looking for behind a letter from a girl. The writing on the scrap of paper said:

"The fight is crossed. We got your father. If you win we will kill him. If you lose we will let him go in fine health."

The shadows of the plot shifted closer to the truth.

Blackstone was waiting in the empty gymnasium when Ebony returned. An oil lamp burned in the changing-room.

Ebony didn't look tired. As if he had run a few hundred yards, then meditated in the shelter of the hedgerow.

Blackstone said, "I know, Ebony."

Ebony stared at him, teeth very white in the lamplight.

Blackstone hit him full in the mouth, knocking him to the floor. Then he left.

Much later Blackstone went to Ebony's room. He knocked on the door and went in. The tin box was packed and Ebony was dressed. He could have been crying: Blackstone wasn't sure. "Sit down, Ebony," he said. "I'm sorry about what I did. But you should have told me—I would have helped you find the old man. Who's behind it?"

"Donnelly," Ebony said.

Blackstone nodded. "Now this is what I'm going to do. I'm going back to London to find him. I want you to go to the fight just as if nothing had happened. If I don't get your father back to you alive then throw the fight. Lose it. To hell with them. There'll be other fights. But if I get him to you I want you to beat the hell out of Houseman. Understood?"

He left before Ebony had time to reply.

171

14

Lawler visited several bookmakers, starting, without much hope, with those in the same circumstances as himself.

They had no business premises and weren't welcomed at Tattersalls. The Fancy only frequented them when their luck was out and their bets were too small for the bigger bookmakers. Lawler and his kind also attracted a few wagers by offering generous odds; but, if luck ran against them, they disappeared as swiftly as the winning racehorse.

Lawler was justified in not being hopeful with his initial inquiries: a five-shilling bet worried his colleagues: £5,000 was the sort of sum nobility left each other in their wills.

Next, he tried the tobacco shops in which lists of runners were posted among the china jars of shag and flake.

In one shop, where the owner was experimenting with a tiny gas-jet with which customers could sample tobacco, Lawler noticed that odds of six to four *on* were being offered for Billy the Butcher.

"You must be cracked," Lawler told the owner, a chubby man with protruding nostril hairs clogged with snuff.

The owner shrugged, polishing the brass rail on the

counter. "There's a lot of blunt gone on the Butcher. Someone must know something."

"But where's it all coming from?"

"From some titled swell, according to all accounts. Maybe he's cracked. I don't know, but I can't afford to take chances." He rubbed hard at the brass, thin from years of polishing. "What do you want anyway—a wager or some baccy?"

"One or the other," Lawler said. "Maybe both." He leaned on the counter. "Any idea who this titled gent is?"

The owner shook his head. "Nor has anyone else. Someone must be putting the brass on for him." He stared at Lawler, trying to categorize him. "Some snuff, perhaps?"

Lawler shook his head. "Not snuff. I don't like it."

"The King takes it," the tobacconist said. "Although," he admitted, "they do say he only pretends to because it's fashionable."

"You would think," Lawler said, "that it would be easy enough to trace this fellow who's putting the money on for him."

"You would think so," the tobacconist agreed. "But if I had a bet I'd put my blunt on the sambo."

"So would I," Lawler said.

"Why don't you then?"

Lawler drummed on his fingers on the brass rail, leaving four prints which the tobacconist removed. "Maybe I will."

"It's a strange fight," the tobacconist said. "Seems to have attracted more attention than the main attraction."

"It's all that money," Lawler said. "And a lot more following it."

"It must be crossed."

"I reckon so." Lawler pointed at the tiny jet of gaslight. "Mind if I sample your own special blend?"

174

"If you're thinking of buying some."

Lawler stuffed a generous portion into his stubby clay pipe. "So you've no idea who's laying the money?"

The tobacconist said, "None at all. Now if you like that particular blend . . ."

"Frankly," Lawler said, heading for the door, "I thought they normally swept this stuff up after the Lord Mayor's Show."

From the tobacconist's Lawler progressed to some of the higher-class bookmakers in the West End. Here his inquiries were less exhausting because the wealthy tended to bet among themselves—settling up at Tattersalls every Monday—and there weren't many bookmakers.

At first the counter clerks, more like bank officials than bookmakers' assistants, treated him with respect. Dress wasn't necessarily a guide to capital among their clientele, and Lawler *was* acting the part of an eccentric gambler. But the part was too much for him, the voice of poverty too loud.

After a while the clerks shook their heads, turned away and nodded at muscular men at the doors. Lawler left quietly, pondering the limits of his chameleon abilities.

With the money which Blackstone had given him burning holes in his pocket, Lawler headed for Bill Richmond's tavern next to the Fives Court.

Richmond, the big Negro from New York who came to England as one of the Duke of Northumberland's servants and won fame for his fighting technique of hitting and getting out of the way, was talking about Ebony Joe's fight.

"I wish," he told a group of the Fancy, "that I was managing him. I'd have done the same for him as I did for Tom Molyneux."

There was a brief silence while the customers remembered. In 1810, advised by Richmond, Molyneux fought Tom Cribb, the champion—and was beaten by the bitter cold. Next year he fought him again, and lost. His next opponent was liquor; and he died in 1818. But, they remembered, nodding over their ale, it *was* Richmond who had made Molyneux the fighter he was. Poor old Snowball, they mourned, drinking his last enemy.

Talk turned to the campaign to stop prizefighting. "They'll never do it," Richmond said in his deep voice. "There's too many in favor of milling. *I* remember Snowball's second fight with Cribb. Every magistrate in Rutland came to see it."

"Maybe," said one of his customers. "But you couldn't say the same in Middlesex or Buckingham."

"Nor Cambridge or Suffolk," said another.

"It's that bastard Blackstone," a man with a thin face said. "It's a wonder no one's done for him."

"Not for the want of trying," said someone else.

Lawler drifted into the group, and didn't demur when Richmond bought a round of drinks and included him. Delicately he steered the talk round to the betting.

But no one knew who had placed the £5,000 bet.

"I know who I'd back," Richmond said.

"And are you backing him?" the thin-faced man asked.

The old fighter shook his head. "Not with all that brass going on the Bristol boy. There's something wrong somewhere."

Lawler allowed them each to buy him a drink, then slid into the night when it was his turn to buy. A few taverns later he found himself in Portland Place.

"You're tipsy," Maisie reproached him. "Fancy visiting a lady in that state. Have you paid?" she asked as he laid himself fully clothed on the bed.

176

Lawler said he had; they had an hour together.

"Lawler," she said.

"Yes?" He put his hands behind his head and stared at his feet, noticing that the sole was leaving the body of one shoe.

"It seems wrong you having to pay like this."

Lawler agreed, not speaking too much because the words rolled out and scattered like marbles.

"I mean we're fond of each other." She paused uncertainly. "Aren't we?"

Lawler didn't reply.

Accepting his silence as an affirmative, she went on, "Maybe if I went on doing this a little longer we could get enough money to rent a place out at Camden Town. You don't want to stay the rest of your life in the Rookery, do you Lawler?"

"Not likely," Lawler said.

"Lawler?"

"Yes?"

"Do you think I could come over to your place one day?"

"I suppose so," said Lawler. He frowned at the thought of his frying pan with its ancient black crusts.

"I could tidy it up for you a bit."

"What makes you think it's untidy?"

She smiled maternally. "I'm sure it is." She stroked his hair. "Lawler," she said, "would you like another name?"

Lawler shrugged, closing his eyes as the ceiling diminished as if he were looking through the wrong end of a telescope.

"Richard Lawler," she said, experimentally. "How's that?"

He thought: Mr. and Mrs. Richard Lawler, more like. It didn't sound too bad—just a little too respectable.

She said, "Or Henry Lawler. Makes you sound a bit like an actor, doesn't it?"

"That's not bad," Lawler admitted.

"Or Edmund Lawler."

Lawler sat up straight, then sank back. "Not Edmund," he muttered. He closed his eyes again. "Let's just leave it at Lawler."

"All right," she said, "if that's the way you want it." She began to unlace his boots.

"Hey," he said, "I've only got three-quarters of an hour left."

"Don't worry," she said. "It's getting late. I doubt if there'll be any more gentlemen tonight. The old bitch downstairs won't mind if you stay the night. She doesn't want to lose me. She knows when she's on to a good thing. A lot of gentlemen come here because of me. . . ."

Lawler's body jerked as if he were in the suburbs of sleep.

Maisie said, "Do you ever get jealous, Lawler?"

"No," Lawler said.

"Never?"

"Never."

"I'd be jealous of you," she said. "If I thought you were going with another girl."

"Come off it," Lawler said, drowsily.

"Do you do a lot of gambling?" She lifted his legs and pulled the blankets over his body; then took off her clothes, designed for easy release, and slipped in beside him, pressing her thin body against his.

"Quite a bit," Lawler said, turning his back on her.

She wound her arms round him. "I've got some news that I've been keeping, Lawler," she said, hoping that it would wake him.

178

"What's that?" His voice was drugged.

"Someone wants to save me."

"Wants to what?"

"To save me. A gentleman wants to save me."

"From what?"

"From all this. This way of life. I was thinking, Lawler, that if I allowed myself to be saved, and this gentleman gave me some money to help me be saved, and then he got me a job in service, perhaps we could settle down somewhere. You know, perhaps you could come and work in the same house."

Lawler turned towards her, a movement which she interpreted as affection "There," she said, "you go to sleep." She cradled his head. "I just thought you might have heard of him," she said, "you being in the gambling business. His name is Cadogan. Sir Humphrey Cadogan, I think. He was a bit drunk. Said he was going to make a lot of money on some prizefight in which one of the fighters —a black boy I think, was deliberately going to lose."

She looked to see if Lawler was interested, but he was asleep.

It was five in the morning when Lawler awoke. It was still dark and Maisie's breathing was deep and rhythmical.

He sat up and shook her awake. "What was that you said?"

"What was what?"

"Just as I was going to sleep you mentioned a name."

"Cadogan?"

"That was it," Lawler swung out his legs and sat on the edge of the bed shivering. "I've got to go."

"Where?"

"Barnet."

179

"What ever for?"

"It doesn't matter."

Maisie began to cry.

He searched for his boots in the dark, pain throbbing in his head.

In between sobs she said, "There isn't a coach to Barnet until this afternoon."

"Are you sure?" He paused, a boot in one hand.

"Of course I'm sure."

"Then there isn't much point in rushing off, I suppose . . ."

"Oh, Lawler," she said. She put her arms round him.

"But I'll have to get there tonight."

"There, there," she said.

"I've just got to."

A little after she said, "Lawler?"

"Yes?"

"You're going to see this Cadogan, aren't you?"

Lawler said he probably was. "What of it?"

"I was just thinking . . . Perhaps you could mention the both of us if he talks about putting me into service."

"Perhaps," Lawler said.

Lawler arrived at Barnet in the evening and went straight to Sir Humphrey Cadogan's mansion. But when he got there he was told that Blackstone had left for London.

15

One man to find in London.

Three days to find him.

One man in any one of the Rookeries scattered beside the bastions of the upper classes and the middle classes. Holborn, Snow Hill, Whitechapel, Old Mint, the Dials. In the warehouses of Shadwell or Wapping; at the "Venice of Drains" in Bermondsey; among the dollyshops of Rosemary Lane; in the tap-rooms of Ratcliffe Highway.

One old blackbird in a capital.

The assignment, Blackstone thought, as he changed in his rooms, had elements of the impossible.

It was 6.30 p.m. The spring day had blown itself away and a night breeze was sniffing the streets. He poured himself a glass of whisky and attended to his guns. Tonight he concentrated on two antique pieces: a 1699 Spanish 12-bore with a barrel by Gaspar Fernandez of Madrid and a Scottish snap-haunce pistol with a Celtic pattern on the barrel, about 1625.

As he worked he planned. First he had to alert his army of informants; fences, footpads, whores, beggars, a cracksman or two, magsmen, hackney drivers, costers. A fat reward promised.

181

Blackstone peered down the barrel of the Spanish gun and found a single thread of cobweb which he removed like a guilty housemaid.

I have one real hope, he thought. Donnelly. If I can find the bastard.

Ebony had mentioned a waterside pub where he met Donnelly: that was where Blackstone had to go first.

He put away the antiques and selected four more lethal guns. And the long French naval dagger which he slid inside his boot.

Then he went out into the fresh young night hunting an old blackbird.

But Donnelly wasn't in the Thames-side inn; nor did anyone recognize his description.

"Keep an eye open," Blackstone told the landlord.

The landlord responded with steady, blue-eyed dishonesty. "That I will, sir," he said.

Where would Donnelly go from here? Blackstone looked up the street, the mossy smell of the river in his nostrils. To the next tavern, he decided, remembering Donnelly's beery face.

He turned down the Ratcliffe Highway where the girls awaited the sailors home from the sea. They laughed a lot, singing shanties, spilling into the night from the rum-reeking tap-rooms, gypsy-bright with ribbons and paper flowers.

Blackstone visited a couple of taverns, noting the shift in atmosphere when he entered. An Irishman named Donnelly? They laughed warily. What sort of a lawman was it that expected you to remember one Irishman in a street of taverns?

He went to a live show above a tap-room featuring a sword-swallower and a singing waiter; he visited an inn frequented by Negro sailors and their newly-found girls, wondering if this was where Ebony had met his dollymop.

No Donnelly.

He rode back to the Brown Bear and asked Ruthven's advice.

Why are you so interested in one old sambo?" Ruthven asked. "I should have thought you had your hands full breaking up this prizefight."

"It's a private investigation," Blackstone said, winking at the serving girl and receiving no response.

Ruthven examined his big fist. "I don't envy you the prizefighting job, Blackie. I like a bit of milling myself. You're not averse either, are you?"

"I don't have any strong feelings about it," Blackstone said, backing away from the shrewdness behind the well-used features.

"Milling will soon be finished as we know it," Ruthven said with regret. "What with Birnie and you and the judges in the courts. It's like everything else—everyone's got too greedy. The fighters, the managers, the villains . . . they reckon this fight with Ebony Joe is crossed." He stared at Blackstone.

Blackstone said, "It's not just greed, George. The Government's scared of any meeting. If they see more than five thousand people they see another French revolution."

"In that case they should ban public executions."

"The anti-milling brigade reckon it teaches our young gentlemen false standards. Apparently all they're talking about at Eton is Ebony Joe versus Housemann."

Ruthven ordered more ale. "It didn't seem to do Wellington much harm. He liked a bit of milling. And," Ruthven said reflectively, "I seem to remember you once saying that you'd done a bit of fighting in your youth."

"So do most boys in the Rookery."

"But you were a bit more than a boy, Blackie." He lit his pipe. "Why don't you own up? Your heart's not in this job, is it?"

"Not particularly," Blackstone said. "Satisfied?"

Ruthven shrugged.

"Now help me find this old man."

"Difficult," Ruthven said, "unless you tell me more about it."

"Not much to tell. He's just an old Negro who's been kidnapped."

"Why in God's name should anyone want to kidnap an old Negro? And why are you so interested?"

"Because," Blackstone said carefully, "he had some information."

"What about? Dosshouses? You'll have to do better than that, Blackie. What's his name, for a start?"

"I don't know."

"Then I can't help you."

"Kentucky," Blackstone said.

"Why," Ruthven said, a smile reaching from his broken nose to his pipe, "that's Ebony Joe's real name, isn't it?"

Blackstone sighed. "He's the boy's father."

"Now," Ruthven said, "we're getting somewhere. Tell me more."

"Strictly between you and me, George?"

Ruthven nodded.

Blackstone told Ruthven most of the story and went home. It was past midnight. Two days to go. One blackbird to find. Two Runners looking for him.

But nothing developed next day.

It was Friday and the fight was on Saturday at Epsom Downs where Tom Cribb once fought Jem Belcher.

184

Ebony's fight was at midday, two hours before the main bout between a Birmingham fighter and a navvy from London's Edgware Road competing for the right to challenge the reigning champion.

Blackstone re-visited his informants, armed with threats and bribes. But no one knew anything about the abduction.

In his pocket the Breguet watch ticked away the hours.

He tried to persuade himself that one crossed fight didn't matter; but he knew it did. If Ebony lost it he, too, was lost because the Fancy had heard rumors. And he would never be matched again.

The Poacher was tiring and Blackstone fed and watered him and let him rest in the stables at Paddington.

Lunch-time. He ate some bread and cheese, drank some ale and caught a hackney to Bow Street where he made the final arrangements to stop the fight.

Birnie seemed satisfied. "You look tired," he observed.

"It's taken a lot of organizing, sir."

Birnie nodded. "Let's hope this will prove that we don't need another police force."

"Let's hope so, sir."

He took another hackney to the fringe of the Rookery and talked with the pieman standing among his sparks.

The pieman shook his head. "No word," he said.

He tried Sol's Arms. The swell mobsmen accepted drinks from him but couldn't help. Barclay even bought a round in commiseration. "It's not our line of territory, Blackie," he said. "We aim a bit higher than old beggars."

"I'll remember that," Blackstone told him.

"Toss you for a sovereign," Barclay said.

Blackstone tossed and lost.

The Breguet ticked away inside its warm gold case.

Blackstone returned to the Soho tavern where Shoe-

185

mark had been murdered. In the ring a young Staffordshire, pink-eyed and almost earless, was being auctioned—as a dog-fighter rather than a ratter. Its ears had been snipped off to remove toothholds and it was sparring with an old battler, almost senile but still possessing instinctive pit skills.

Blackstone didn't recognize any of the bidders. No overgrown thumb-nail on the ring.

The landlord said, "Not more questioning."

"Not this time," Blackstone said. "But I'll be back."

"You don't still think I had anything to do with it, do you? Why the hell should I get rid of the best source of rats in London?"

"There must be a worthy successor to King Rat's throne somewhere," Blackstone said.

"There are several contenders. But they're not in the same class. Sewer rats are the best they can find. I had a reputation for barn rats. That's why everyone came here. Now business is falling off."

Blackstone said, "He certainly had a way with rats, did Shoemark."

"That he did. They do say"—the landlord leaned forward confidentially—"they do say that when they buried him a dozen rats jumped in the grave with him."

A deal was concluded beside the ring and the Staffordshire was lifted out in disgrace because of its reluctance to savage the old warrior.

Without much hope, Blackstone asked the landlord if he knew anything about the disappearance of the old man.

His lack of hope was justified.

He caught another hackney carriage back to Bow Street. He felt he had betrayed the Bow Street Runners, Ebony Joe and himself.

Perhaps the old man was dead, his body dumped in the Thames. Unlikely, though, because the kidnappers might have been forced to produce him alive to convince Ebony that he had to lose the fight.

Blackstone paid the driver and went into the Brown Bear. He was exhausted. And looked it because the girl said, "Has the Honorable Miss Cadogan been keeping you up late?"

He didn't reply. He sat at the window, staring across the street at the lighted office where Birnie sat working late.

The exhaustion didn't last long.

George Ruthven came in and said, "There you are."

"Here I am," Blackstone said.

"Donnelly will be at the Daffy Club at nine," Ruthven said.

Donnelly was sitting at one end of the long table talking expansively to the commissary taking the ring to Epsom Downs text day, a sly, bleary man accompanied by a bulldog.

Ruthven said, "You go round one side, I'll go the other."

They had almost reached Donnelly when he spotted them.

He reacted quickly with ancient prize-ring instincts, making for the door shouting, "Save me from Blackstone, lads—the bastard who wants to stop the fight tomorrow."

The crowd thickened around Blackstone. He tried to reach a pistol but they pressed his arms to his sides.

Ruthven barged on, leaving aggrieved bodies behind him.

Donnelly, almost at the door, shouted, "He's another of Blackstone's cronies. Another Bow Street bastard."

The Fancy tried to get in Ruthven's way but most of them went underfoot. He reached the door seconds after Donnelly had left.

Blackstone freed his baton and cracked a couple of skulls. The Fancy fell back. Blackstone pulled a Manton out and someone shouted, "He's got a barker."

Blackstone leapt on the table and ran down it. Ruthven was standing outside, pistol in hand. "He can't have gone far," he said.

The Holborn street was quiet, alive in the darkness beyond the gas-light. A cluster of children sat at the base of one street lamp, sharing body warmth; a blind beggar tapped his way over the cobblestones; three horses were tethered outside another tavern up the street.

Blackstone asked the children, "Did you see anyone come out?"

They shook their heads, faces pale in the gas-light and not much rosier by daylight.

Blackstone tossed them some coins. "Sure?"

They scrambled for the money. One of them, coin in hand, said, "A man went up there, mister." Pointing towards the horses.

Donnelly emerged from the shadows, jumped on a horse which he had untethered, and galloped away.

Blackstone aimed his pistol and fired. The horse reared, then galloped on and the explosion chased itself down the street, the ball snuffing out a gas lamp.

Blackstone ran to the horses, just beating Ruthven.

Donnelly was rounding a corner, heading for the Rookery. Once there he was safe.

Blackstone shouted, "Stop thief." One or two shadows took human form and gave chase. Shout that out in the Rookery and they'd attack the pursuer.

Donnelly turned right, sparks flying from the horse's hoofs. Some way behind, Blackstone could hear Ruthven, a large man on a small horse.

They were out of the gas-light now, torches burning at intervals, candles in the windows. Blackstone urged his horse on: the distance between him and Donnelly shortened.

The stars were hidden and light rain was polishing the cobbles. Twice Blackstone's horse slipped. A hundred yards between them. Less. He raised the other pistol and fired.

Again Donnelly's horse reared. This time its hoofs slipped and it fell, throwing Donnelly.

He stood for a moment, stunned, then ran down an alley towards the Rookery.

Blackstone tried to follow on horseback, but the alley was too narrow. He dismounted and ran after Donnelly, the sound of their footsteps lingering between the leaning buildings.

Blackstone knew there was an escape route into—or out of—the Rookery at the end of the alley. It went through a dismal brothel where opium was smoked, through a chain of cellars and over some well-trodden rooftops, into the heart of the Rookery.

Blackstone grinned. Because if Donnelly was taking that route he was making a mistake: any child of the Rookery, of which Blackstone was one, knew that pathway.

Donnelly vanished into the brothel.

Blackstone waited outside for a few moments. Then went down the alley, cut across two more, kicked open the door of a crouching building and stuffed with old clothes collected by a gang of beggars, and headed for the cellars.

A single torch burned in each cellar, a generous gesture

to fugitives. Blackstone heard Donnelly approaching, two or three cellars away.

He stepped behind an arch, priming the Manton.

Donnelly stumbled past, one hand to his eyes as if he were expecting a bright light. He paused, listening for sounds of pursuit. He sighed deeply when he heard nothing. He leaned against the wall, one hand at his chest feeling his heart.

Blackstone said, "Just stay there, Donnelly, nice and relaxed."

Donnelly screamed.

Blackstone stuck the barrel of the gun in his spine and searched his pockets with his free hand. He found an aged flintlock and threw it into a corner. "Now turn round."

Donnelly turned. "What do you want?"

"You know what I want."

Donnelly's hand returned to his chest. "A pain," he said. "A pain right there."

"Where's the old man?"

"What old man?"

"You know which old man. Where is he, Donnelly?"

"I don't feel well," Donnelly said.

"I'm sure the old man doesn't feel well either." Blackstone wondered if Donnelly was acting.

"I don't know what you're talking about."

Blackstone hit him in the mouth. "Where is he?"

"I don't know."

"But you know what I'm talking about."

Donnelly shook his head. "I need a doctor."

"You'll need an undertaker if you don't tell me where the old man is."

"If you kill me you'll never find him."

"I won't kill you instantly," Blackstone assured him.

"That won't help you. I've been beaten up too many times in the ring."

Blackstone hit him again. "Where is he?" The blood trickling from Donnelly's mouth looked black in the torchlight.

"Find out for yourself."

"I'll find out from you, culley."

Donnelly's hand went to his chest again. "The pain," he said. "There's a terrible pain . . . get me a doctor," he sobbed.

Blackstone said, "Tell me where the old man is and then I'll get you a doctor."

Donnelly leaned against the wall breathing quickly. "You promise?"

"I promise."

"He's in a cellar at Wapping." Donnelly gave Blackstone a street number. "Now get me a doctor."

He slid down the wall on to the floor. Blackstone bent down and listened for his heart. But Donnelly hadn't been acting.

Ruthven was waiting with two of the horses outside the undisturbed brothel. Donnelly's had disappeared.

Ruthven said, "Wapping's a long way. You're exhausted as it is, Blackie."

Blackstone mounted his horse. "I've got to get there."

They trotted down the alley, one behind the other.

Ruthven said, "Even if we find the old man alive you've still got to get him to the fight. How the hell can you manage that in your condition?"

"I'll manage it."

The light rain had been bowled away by the wind and the moon was high and bright. Highwaymen weather.

"I'll get him for you," Ruthven said.

A cat squawked down the alley pursued by a man with a sack. He slowed down when he saw the two horsemen. "There goes another fur stole for my wife," Ruthven said.

Ahead lay a wider street, the moonlight slithering around its cobbles. "No, George," Blackstone said, "you can't do it."

"Why not?"

"Because it's my responsibility." He grinned. "Also you don't know where the fight's taking place."

"It's Epsom Downs. Everyone knows that." He paused. "I hope you weren't thinking of pretending you believed any false venue put out by the Fancy?"

Blackstone admitted he had been at one time.

"You must be mad. Birnie would never fall for that. Nor would anyone else. The Runners would be a laughing stock and you'd be playing right into the hands of Peel."

Blackstone urged his horse into a canter. "I know," he said. "I realize that now."

Ruthven cantered beside him. They were back in the gaslight, a sickly glow compared with moonlight.

Ruthven raised his voice as the night air flowed past them. "What are you going to do? As far as I can see you're racing to Wapping to get the old man so that Ebony Joe can win his fight. At the same time you're duty bound to break it up. Am I right, Blackie?"

"You're right," Blackstone agreed.

They reached the tavern where the horses had been tethered. There was a knot of people outside excitedly discussing horse thieves. Ruthven told them where to look for the third horse and said, "A drink before we go to Wapping, Blackie?"

"A drink before *I* go."

"I'm coming with you. I want to see how you're going to deal with this."

They took a hackney to Bow Street, borrowed a couple of horses and headed for Wapping.

The address was a warehouse filled with crates of fruit —oranges mostly, judging by the smell. The shippers must have miscalculated the ripening because the smell had a rotting, jungle quality.

Blackstone and Ruthven reined in their horses at the end of the quay. The tide was out and the sails of the ships riding the dark water, scattered with coins of moonlight, were furled.

A rowing boat thrust an arrow across the water and the moonlight scattered. Despite the flapping of a loose sail, the creaking of masts, the distant splash of oars, there was an immensity of silence in this place: the tall ships home from chaotic ports, piracy and wild smuggling nights were at rest.

The two Runners stood on the quayside smelling the muddy breeze; talking in whispers; aware of undefined nocturnal fear.

Blackstone said, "You go round the front, I'll take the waterside. Donnelly said there were two guards."

They checked their guns.

Ruthven crept towards the front entrance of the warehouse, keeping in the shadows; a puny figure beneath the big watching buildings.

Blackstone climbed down an iron ladder, feeling the rust flake away in his hands. One foot touched the mud. A couple of rats darted away. He seemed to have been keeping company with a lot of rats lately.

Gun in hand he edged along the mud under the lips of

the warehouses. The smell of rotting oranges grew stronger.

He stopped directly under the warehouse and listened. Silence.

He took another step and slipped on a heap of oranges, feeling them split softly under his boots.

Footsteps. Slow and tentative. Probably Ruthven, never noted for ballet graces. The creak of a door far away.

Between Blackstone's head and the landing-stage was a grill. Cautiously he tested it; it was firm in the wall.

He pulled himself up and peered through the iron bars.

And saw the whites of a man's eyes, a tooth or two. Nothing else—which led him to suspect that the rest of the face was black.

He lowered himself back to the mud.

Across the river the skyline was beginning to pale. He looked at his watch. Six-thirty. In five and a half hours Ebony Joe would be coming up to the scratch.

He found a slimy rope and began to haul himself up to the landing-stage, bouncing against the wall, finishing off his boots, slipping back one foot for every two he climbed.

Sweat trickled into his eyes. A clock chimed.

Then he was on the landing-stage, aware that he was silhouetted against the freshening sky.

Someone else was also aware.

The explosion lit the cathedral spaces of the warehouse and the ball seared the shoulder of his top coat. He flung himself to one side, landing in juicy pulp.

Another explosion, Ruthven firing, Blackstone guessed.

The plumage of silence settled again.

Someone had to make a move. Either that or they would stay there until daylight.

Blackstone pushed a crate and stared into the darkness

as it toppled, hit the landing-stage and fell into the mud. A reflex movement to the right. He fired, forgetting until he had pulled the trigger that it might be Ruthven.

A cry of pain. A sob.

Blackstone shouted, "Are you all right, George?"

"I'm all right."

Another explosion as someone shot in the direction of Ruthven's voice. Blackstone dived, pistol in one hand, French dirk in the other.

The man was powerful, foul-breathed, unshaven. He clubbed at Blackstone with his pistol, catching him on the shoulder. They broke and stood up, vague shapes, the oranges mashed to marmalade at their feet.

The man lunged. Blackstone side-stepped, pushing him on to complete his lunge. Then threw himself on the man's body finding his throat, pressing the blade of the dirk into his windpipe. "One more squirm out of you, culley, and I'll slit your throat." He shouted to Ruthven, "I've got one. The other's yours." He pricked his man's throat. "Tell your friend to give himself up."

The man shouted to the other guard, but there was no reply.

Blackstone heard Ruthven making his way through the crates. Then he called out, "It's all right, Blackie, he's dead. My shot must have got him."

In the cellar, as the new light found its way through the bars, the old man grinned gratefully. As he had grinned ever since he was a fledgling blackbird.

They rode their tired horses through the countryside south of London. It was a bright expectant morning, spring scents released by wind and rain; a rehearsal for summer; a fine day for a fight.

195

Ruthven said, "We'll have to change the horses soon." He looked at Blackstone. "We should be changing you as well. You look as if you're all in."

"I'm all right," Blackstone lied. When the horses slowed to a trot he fell asleep in the saddle, the old man cuddled in front of him.

They went to a village inn where Ruthven ordered porridge, ham and eggs, muffins and tea, and sent the innkeeper to find fresh horses.

"We can't stop," Blackstone said, rubbing his face, feeling the tiredness printed on it.

"Do you want to get the old man to Epsom alive?"

Blackstone watched Kentucky senior stumble across the room. "I forgot," he said. "I'm sorry."

"Blackstone sorry? You must be tired," Ruthven said.

"Do you think we'll make it?"

"No," Ruthven told him.

A coach was leaving the village, the last stop before London. Boys watered and swept the courtyard. The horses pawed the cobblestones impatiently; the passengers nodded and yawned. A villager tried to sell the passengers oranges.

"I never want to see another orange," Ruthven said. He tackled his porridge as if it were soup, his ham as if he were a butcher.

Blackstone lay back in his chair and slept, food uneaten. Ebony's father ate half his breakfast and wrapped the remainder in a red and white spotted handkerchief.

Ruthven said, "Do you know why you were taken prisoner?"

The old man shook his head.

196

"Don't you want to know?"

The old man grinned at him.

"You know your son's fighting today?"

The old man nodded and made one of his rare speeches. "He's a good boy," he said. "I wish him luck."

Ruthven looked at his watch "He needs more than luck," he said.

The inkeeper arrived; a tyrant with his servants, a sycophant in the presence of two batons with gilt crowns. He had found two horses, he said, and at considerable expense had persuaded their owners to hire them out; they weren't the best horses in the neighborhood but they were the best he could find at such short notice. He hoped they would suit the purposes of such eminent guests, he added, looking doubtfully at Ebony's father. Wouldn't a postchaise have been more suitable for the three of them?

"Not enough time," Ruthven said.

He woke Blackstone.

Blackstone looked at his watch. "Two hours to go," he said. "Do you still think we won't make it?"

"Yes," Ruthven said, "I still think we won't make it."

As they left, the villager tried to sell them oranges and was surprised at the vehemence with which they rejected them.

16

In two minutes Ebony Joe had to come up to the scratch.

Standing in his corner, with his bottleman and kneeman and the old bruiser from Cadogan's gymnasium acting as his manager, he shivered despite the sun directly overhead.

He wore his silk colors made at Spitalfields—light blue with dark blue spots—at waist and knee. Houseman's colors were Bristol yellow. A gentle breeze moved the colors tied to the ropes with seaweed movements.

Houseman lounged against the ropes, waist thick for a young man, butcher's hands hanging heavily from strong arms. Head big with all the blunt been laid on him, Ebony thought.

In the outer ring the old fighters belabored intruders but the pressure from the crowd behind was growing. Some thirty-thousand spectators, Ebony's bottleman estimated, despite the threat from Bow Street. Perhaps some had come to tell their grandchildren of the day they fought the Dragoons (of whom there was no sign).

Ebony watched Hansom tussling with a young blade who fancied himself. If things had been different Ebony would have climbed over the ropes and sparred with

Hansom, the old pug who had launched him. The crowd would have liked that; establishing himself as a character, before he beat the daylights out of Billy the Butcher. But things weren't different and Hansom would shortly see him beaten.

Ebony searched the crowd for the gummy old face of his father.

Nothing.

Behind the crowd on the grassy mound overlooking the race-course, a German band was playing; the crashing of drum and cymbals throbbing above all other noise. Beside the race-course, a green canal of young grass, a grandstand had been built—"Seats 10s. a head" said a contradictory notice. It was packed and swaying slightly. Children waited underneath for coins as spectators rich enough to afford 10s. fumbled for snuff, tobacco, watches.

Tobacco smoke drifted above the crowd like tendrils of blue sky, all part of this summer prelude. The whole scene cosseted in its own smell—chopped grass, mud, tobacco, hot pies and ale.

There were frequent incidents.

At the back of the grandstand, which had now developed a list, a macer working the three-card trick was caught and kicked to death.

"He's spreading the broads," a loser shouted.

Patently this was so: a macer was a macer and it was up to you to be a bit sharper than him. But the accusation in the loser's voice appealed. The boots, some with iron between the soles, went in, and the macer died with his broads.

The crowd pressed forward until the outer ring looked as if it might be engulfed. "Just like Scroggins versus Turner," said the authorities from their safe seats, recalling the chaotic fight in 1817.

200

A pieman's stove caught fire and several children burned their fingers snatching meals from the greasy flames.

A pickpocket found himself picking an accomplice's pocket.

A couple of magistrates took up their positions doing passable imitations of the scoundrels they usually convicted.

The Duke of Clarence, heir to the throne, was said to have come, and gone when he heard about the Bow Street moves.

The referee took his place in the outer ring and was hit by a clod of turf on the back of his neck.

A badger being baited by a snarling dog who really had nothing against badgers finally acknowledged defeat and let himself be killed.

Ebony said to the bottleman, once a promising fighter defeated by his appetite for food, "Any sign of the Dragoons?"

"None," the bottleman said happily. "Looks as if the Fancy's foiled Blackstone and his cronies."

"How could they have done that?"

"Told him to go to the wrong place, I reckon." The plump bottleman took a draft from the bottle. "You wouldn't think he'd be so stupid, would you?"

"No," Ebony said, "you wouldn't." He shivered again, watching the muscles in his belly flicker.

"But in any case the Fancy's got his measure even if he does bring in the military."

"How?" Ebony asked.

"They've got ropes right round the place," the bottleman told him. "Hidden in the grass and the bushes. If the Dragoons attack they'll jerk them up and trip the horses. There are also a lot of murderous coves waiting for them,

with sticks and clubs and a barker or two, I shouldn't
wonder. The Dragoons won't be expecting anything like
that. Why should they? No one's ever counter-attacked
before. And there'll only be a few of them. Compared with
the Fancy that is," the bottleman said, pointing at the
crowds.

"Where are the ropes then?"

"In a circle," the bottleman said. "The bushes make a
sort of circle, don't they? Not that it matters," he said,
taking another swig of Ebony's bottle. "I reckon Blackstone's got cold feet."

The kneeman said, "Take it easy at first, Ebony. Make
it look like a fight. You've got two hours. Finish him off
just before two o'clock."

Across the ring Houseman did some jogging, taking a
couple of swings at no one; Ebony noticed the flesh on his
hips jogging with him. Did he have to get beaten by this
fleshy thug? Absent toothless gums answered in the affirmative.

Blackie, where are you?

The kneeman, an older man with a curiously bent nose,
confided, "There's been a lot of talk about this fight,
Ebony."

"I know," Ebony said. "They say it's crossed."

"It made me laugh," said the kneeman, feeling the angle
of his nose.

"And me," said the bottleman.

They waited.

When Ebony didn't reply the bottleman said, "We've
put quite a lot of brass on you, Ebony."

Ebony said, "You'll get a fight for your money."

"We don't want a fight, Ebony. We want a victory."

He wanted to tell them to cancel their bets. Back the

fat butcher's boy. Put everything you've got on him. Become rich and escape from this rotten sport where even a straight left is crooked.

He searched the crowd.

One black face in the white hordes. That was all he wanted. Nothing.

And I believed in you, Blackstone. Mister Blackstone. Ever since that day in Paddington when we put the gloves on. . . .

The seconds tossed, Ebony won. He chose the corner facing the least distracting section of the crowd.

At least, he thought, let me show that I can fight. Although he had to be careful not to hurt Houseman too much: he didn't look too game and if he retired hurt then his father was a dead man.

The first round lasted two minutes twenty seconds according to the two umpires. It ended when Houseman took a cleaving swing at Ebony, missed and fell.

According to the rules a round could only end if a fighter was felled by a blow. But the end of the round was called and Ebony's supporters cried out, "Foul."

The crowd surged forward, pushing the swells in front of them. The pickpockets went gratefully to work.

For one frightening moment Ebony imagined himself winning on a foul. But it was unlikely. The Fancy hadn't come all this way to see a fight—even a supporting bout— won with a foul.

Another clod of earth hit the referee on the head.

Ebony took a swig from his bottle containing sugared water laced with brandy.

"You'll have him hanging in his butcher's shop with all the other carcasses," the bottleman said happily.

"I'm already spending my blunt," said the kneeman.

Ebony shivered.

"What's the matter?" the bottleman asked. "Warm enough for you, isn't it?"

"Yes," Ebony said, "it's warm enough."

He took another drink from the bottle and went up to the scratch, both fists held out in front. Rigid—just as Blackstone had taught him not to stand.

He experimented with some footwork, ducked, feinted, knuckled Houseman's cheeks a couple of times. Houseman caught him a clubbing blow on the side of the head. Ebony was glad in a way: at least he wouldn't lose to a total amateur.

Houseman's supporters cheered. "Now a couple of rib-roasters, Billy boy. Rattle his ivories—he's got enough of them."

Ebony landed a squashing blow on Houseman's nose.

"Good old Ebony. Any claret yet? Has he tapped the Butcher's ruby?"

Ebony tasted blood; but it was only from a bite on his tongue. Keep this up, hurting each other but not too much, because there was always a chance that Blackstone might make it. He shook his head—no chance—and took a punch on the jaw.

"That's it, Billy boy. That's it, me bold Butcher. Give him a bash. Give him a knock-downer."

Ebony blinked, swayed to one side and felt his knuckles jolt against the Butcher's teeth. Not too hard, Kentucky. Watch yourself. Put the Butcher down for good and you'll never see your father again.

A trickle of blood oozed from Houseman's mouth.

The Fancy, quick to spot such evidence, let out a howl. "Ebony's tapped his claret for him. First blood to Ebony."

Ebony felled Houseman with a flat-fisted blow to the

side of the face which would give him thirty seconds to recover.

He went back to his second's knee.

They were singing on the improvised grandstand, swaying backwards and forwards, passing bottles around. The grandstand took up the rhythm of it; lurched to one side and failed to right itself.

The laughter froze.

A creak and a groan of wounded metal and wood.

The children underneath ran for it.

The occupants slid to one side. Wood snapped with pistol shots and five hundred of the Fancy crashed into the mud. There was a lot of shrieking, a lot of moaning, much confirmation of imminent death. But when they were sorted out there were only three broken legs, two broken arms and a dozen cracked ribs.

Ebony thought: another reprieve. He searched the spectators again. No father. No Blackstone.

They took two of the wounded away; the rest stayed, nursing their crooked limbs.

Round Three. There appeared to be some concern in Houseman's camp. One of his seconds tried to distract Ebony, and once he got in the way of a punch Ebony aimed at Houseman's face.

As they wrestled in a corner Houseman's knee jolted into Ebony's groin. The pain was the thrust of a knife, and he thought he was going to vomit.

Ebony remembered Blackstone's words: "Don't let the lout get close. He's stronger than you. Keep your distance. Make a fool of him. And for God's sake don't let him get you in chancery."

Ebony ducked away, loins aching. If he became too angry he would put Houseman down for good. He let go two punches, one bringing blood from Houseman's nose, the other opening a small cut above his eye.

The Fancy applauded. "He'll have a lovely mouse there, Ebony."

"Come on, Billy," shouted a wit, "give him a white eye."

Houseman came at Ebony with his head down, trying to butt him. Ebony stepped aside, driving his knuckles into the lowered face. The blow jolted Houseman backwards and he fell on his back, showing no inclination to get up again.

Ebony stood over him. "Get up," he said. "For God's sake get up." He was trembling.

Houseman had his eyes closed but Ebony sensed that he was shamming. He kicked him. "Get up, culley, or I'll tread on your throat."

The butcher stirred.

The Fancy were displeased with Houseman. A few missiles sailed into the ring. Someone got hold of the German band's big drum and began to beat it. "Coward, coward, coward," bayed the crowd.

"Get up," Ebony whispered. "Please get up."

Houseman opened his eyes, slyness beneath the lids. "Why do you want me up, Ebony?"

"Just get up."

Slowly Houseman stood up, puffed lips grinning. "So it's true is it?" He spat in Ebony's face. "Next round you fall, eh? Next round you take a clout in the face and maybe a butt in the belly. Right?"

Ebony returned to his corner. Sir Humphrey Cadogan was standing in the outer ring, noble features worried. He acknowledged Ebony with a wave of his cane.

The bottleman said, "You've got him beat, Ebony."

The kneeman extended a thick thigh and said, "This is

my last fight. My wife's always cursed milling. She won't any more—I'm buying a cottage in the country at Fulham."

"Have you got a lot of money on me?" Ebony asked.

"Everything," the kneeman said.

A tall man with a smallpoxed face detached himself from the spectators and came into the outer ring. Hansom went up to him belligerently; money changed hands and the man came up to the ropes, beckoning Ebony.

"Where's Donnelly?" he asked.

"I don't know," Ebony said. "Who are you?"

"It doesn't matter who I am." The man's fingers fluttered around the pock-marks. "I represent the same interests as Donnelly. Understand?"

"I suppose so."

"You're fighting a little too boldly, aren't you, culley?" He had a Welsh accent, voice dipping into the valleys.

"Houseman's fighting badly," Ebony said.

"Then you'd better fight worse. Much worse." He paused. Then, realizing that the interval was almost over, added, "Your old man's quite well, Ebony. Eating well. Breathing well. You want him to go on breathing, don't you?"

Ebony started shivering again.

"Well, don't you?"

Ebony nodded.

"Fight worse then. Only don't make it too obvious. Another half-hour will do it nicely." He smiled. "All right?"

Ebony nodded.

"This evening," said the Welshman, turning to go, "you'll find the old man back in his room in Camden Town. As long as you don't get too bold."

The kneeman said, "Who was that, Ebony?"

207

"No one that matters."

"You're shivering again."

The bottleman gave him some nectar. "This'll warm you up."

Round Four. Ebony loosed a left at Houseman—and Houseman's second parried it. The Fancy screamed abuse while the grinning second indicated that it had been an accident.

"Get back a bit," Houseman said softly, sniffing blood.

Ebony pretended to try and dodge. Houseman's head caught him in the belly, then cracked into his face.

Ebony creased forwards, fell sideways. You bastard, he thought. Oh you bastard. The vomit rose but he fought it back. One day I'll kill you, Butcher's boy. One day a butcher's knife in that big thick belly.

Houseman stood over him. "Get up," he said. "Please get up." He grinned and kicked Ebony in the kidneys.

"Foul," cried Ebony's supporters.

"Coward," cried Houseman's supporters.

The breeze had quickened, making the colors on the ropes flap. The drum and cymbals were going again.

Ebony stood up shaking his head. The muscles in his belly were knotted and he could move one tooth with his tongue.

"You was a bit slow that time," the bottleman said. "Never mind—you can't win every round. Otherwise you'd make it look too easy, wouldn't you?" he queried hopefully.

"But you can't take too much of that treatment," the kneeman observed as the cottage in Fulham receded minimally.

"I'm sorry," Ebony said.

"For what?"

"Just sorry."

He searched the crowd. Drank some potion. Kneaded his stomach with his fingers to untie the knots. Smelt the fire and the sizzling herrings and heard the applause of the patrons at the dosshouse in St. Giles.

Round Five. Ebony avoided as much punishment as possible. But the blow in the stomach had slowed him down; the pain stayed there and the knots tied up his breathing. After a minute he took a flabby punch on the cheek and fell for a thirty-second break.

The fighters in the main bout had arrived and were sitting with the swells in the outer ring. The Birmingham navvy, massive, knock-kneed, stripped for battle beneath a top coat; the London boxer smaller, deceptively benign and bow-legged.

Round Six. Houseman got Ebony in a bear-hug. "Fall, black boy," he grunted. He heaved but Ebony stayed upright. "Fall or I'll get my seconds to throw in the sponge. You wouldn't like that, would you?"

Ebony fell and Houseman crashed on top of him. The breath sighed from Ebony's lungs.

Ebony's seconds didn't speak when he got back to his corner. They know, he thought. They know.

Round Seven. Ebony made a show of it, bringing up pink blotches on Houseman's ribs, tapping another vintage of claret from his nose.

Round Eight. Ebony paid for round seven. Houseman got him in chancery—head under his arm—and pumped in punches. When he let him go Houseman grinned and said, "Pity I can't get you by that hair of yours, eh, Ebony?"

The seconds were bleak; the cottage in Fulham in ruins. The bottleman wiped Ebony's forehead and squeezed cold water over his face. He held the sponge. "Shall I throw this in the next round?"

Not this one, Ebony thought. The next one perhaps,

because I can't take much more. Then I'll seek refuge in the Rookery. Disappear. He saw himself in twenty years' time, with his begging bowl, clutching at passing ankles, the plea and the gratitude folded eternally on his face.

Round Nine. Houseman whispered, "The next round, Ebony. My fists are getting wore out hitting you."

There wasn't much action and the Fancy showed its displeasure. The referee dodged another clod of earth.

A few white clouds had assembled and the sun was just beginning its descent. A fine tranquil afternoon ahead for the main battle and the exit from prizefighting of Ebony Joe Kentucky after a career of extreme brevity.

Houseman tried to throw him; Ebony assisted him by buckling at the knees and falling.

The spectators expressed disgust. "Why didn't you bring a bed? Get him a cushion. someone. It's a carve-up for the Butcher. Get him a knife."

The bottleman finished the contents of the bottle without handing it to Ebony. The kneeman kept his knee to himself. Sir Humphrey Cadogan smiled. The Welshman with the pock-marked face nodded, hands still at his craters.

Drums banging, cymbals crashing . . . herrings cooking, disapproval on the faces of po-faced benefactors, his father's stupid face near the incandescent stove . . . Blackstone knocking him down with kindly fists. . .

Time was called.

"This round?" the bottleman asked, holding up the sponge.

The big man with the tired battered face who had just come into the outer ring said, "I don't think so, culley."

And his father said, "Give it to him, son." Grinning and

pleading there in the afternoon sunshine. Such a stupid face.

"All right," Houseman said, "this is it."

"Is it?" But Ebony's arms were heavy, his belly knotted, his groin aching, his breath lodged in his lungs.

He looked behind to make sure—there was the black face peering through the ropes—and took a blow on the neck.

He saw the bottleman raising the sponge.

"Is it?" Ebony repeated.

Houseman charged with the guile of a butting ram. Ebony danced to one side, as lightly as his heavy feet would allow, and Billy the Butcher charged on, falling against the ropes.

Laughter from the Fancy.

Houseman said, "I'm warning you . . ."

"Don't fall," Ebony said. "Please don't fall yet."

"All right," Houseman breathed, coming at Ebony, trying to push him against the ropes.

It had to be now. Ebony ducked, slammed in a punch just below the ribs; swayed and got another in to the neck; feinted and closed up Houseman's other eye.

All noise was suspended. All movement stopped, save for the flurrying black fists in the ring.

To the nose, the eyes, the ribs, the belly.

Houseman tried to speak, spitting out a tooth. Shaking his head. Trying to fall but Ebony holding him against the ring.

Houseman appealed to his seconds: they looked at the white clouds assembling.

Nose, eyes, ribs, belly.

One voice cracked the silence. Then everyone was shouting, crying, waving their fists as they joined Ebony in his massacre; even those wounded when the grandstand collapsed forgot their broken limbs.

Houseman's mouth hung open, his eyes stared beyond Ebony.

A strange emotion assailed Ebony. He didn't analyze it then; but subsequently he puzzled over it. Whatever it was, it made him drop his fists and allow Houseman to slide down the ropes to the ground.

The pock-faced Welshman said, "You'll pay for this, Kentucky." The big, gruff man whose name was Ruthven said, "So will you," and snapped handcuffs on the Welshman's wrists.

The kneeman offered his knee again and the bottleman said he was off to Fulham in the morning.

A collection was organized for Houseman, who would live to carve another joint, Ebony was told.

Sir Humphrey Cadogan left thoughtfully.

The referee said he was damned if he was going to have anything to do with another fight.

Ebony said to his father, "What did you think of that, then?"

His father handed the cold breakfast wrapped in his handkerchief to Ebony. "You must be hungry," he said.

17

The Dragoons arrived at the assembly point at 1.30. By 1.35 they were trotting briskly along the road towards the prize-ring two miles away.

Blackstone went into the ring at 1.45, raising one hand to acknowledge the disbelief and consternation among the spectators.

He shouted, but his voice didn't carry beyond the swells in their white box-coats. The message was transmitted swiftly up and around the hill.

"Gentlemen, I'm sorry to have to do this. But the law is the law and it's my duty to enforce it. The main fight will *not* take place."

"It's already taken place," someone shouted, to the displeasure of the two principal antagonists who had just thrown their hats into the ring.

Blackstone grinned. "So please go home. I repeat—the fight will not take place."

"Who's going to stop it?" A voice from the navigator's camp.

There was £300 a side at stake, the money having been deposited at a sporting dinner a week earlier.

Not to be outdone, a member of the Londoner's camp

shouted, "Yes, who's going to stop it? Not Blackstone the Runner, I'll wager."

Blackstone's nerves twitched in his exhausted limbs. "Not only Blackstone the Runner," he shouted, pointing at the skyline.

The Dragoons were spaced out with drilled precision; toy silhouettes in the sunlight; steel and brass capturing nuggets of sunlight.

There were a few knowing smiles.

"So you think they'll win the day for you, Blackstone?"

"Chuck him out of the ring."

One of the navigator's seconds who had once fought Dutch Sam rushed Blackstone, fists waving. Blackstone put him down with one punch.

Blackstone gave a magician's wave with his baton. "No fight," he said. "I'm sorry."

The two fighters entered the ring.

Blackstone fired his pistol.

The Dragoons started forward; silhouettes swelling. Then they stopped.

Blackstone, who had heard about the ropes and the ambush from Ebony and relayed the information to the officer in charge, waited.

So did the Fancy.

The Dragoons dismounted. They slashed at the encircling bushes with their swords, then remounted.

The horses broke into a canter. Riders in blue and grey, blades of sunlight gripped in their hands.

The Fancy began to withdraw. To retreat. To flee.

Blackstone looked at his Breguet. Two o'clock: the time he had said he would break up the fighting.

Birnie said, "Very commendable, I suppose."

Blackstone thanked him and took some snuff.

"There are one or two aspects that still puzzle me."

"Really, sir?"

"Why didn't you stop the supporting bout between the black boy and the Bristol butcher?"

Blackstone shrugged. "The main object, sir, was to prevent the big fight. To break up the meeting. I did exactly that."

"The black boy won, I believe. In rather odd circumstances."

On Birnie's desk was a letter bearing Peel's signature. Blackstone suspected it was a letter of commendation. The Fieldings looked complacent on the wall.

Blackstone said, "So I believe."

"Everyone thought he had lost. Then he made a remarkable recovery. Were you there?"

"I was with the Dragoons, sir."

"But you did go into the ring."

"I had to warn the Fancy."

"Ruthven also turned up, I understand."

"He offered to help me," Blackstone said. "In his own time."

Birnie sat back thoughtfully while a clerk brought tea. He went on, "Kentucky's recovery seems to have coincided with Ruthven's arrival."

Blackstone sipped his tea.

Birnie said, "Why didn't Ruthven stop that particular fight?"

"The mob would have killed him. He had to wait for the Dragoons and they weren't due till two."

"I see. And why did you choose to arrive two hours

after the first fight? You did explain but I didn't quite follow . . ."

Lies in Birnie's presence were always lonely: squirming silver fish alone in a net.

"Perhaps," Birnie coaxed, "you didn't know about the supporting bout."

"You have to send an explanation, sir?"

Birnie nodded. "That would be it, wouldn't it, Blackstone? The Fancy"—distaste on his tongue—"supplied you with false information about the venue of the fight. But Bow Street isn't fooled as easily as that, is it?"

"We're not easy to fool," Blackstone said.

Birnie said, "So you made your own inquiries." He paused to light his pipe—the churchwarden this morning. "I suppose you had to meet many unsavory contacts to get the correct information. There's a lot of criticism," he explained, "about the people the Runners mix with. Mobsmen in Sol's Tavern and suchlike." Blackstone wondered if he spotted a smile; he wasn't sure—you had to be so quick with Birnie's smiles. "And then," Birnie continued, "you discovered that the correct venue was Epsom Downs. You were told that the fight was at two o'clock and you presumed the beginning of the whole sporting occasion. . . . Am I correct, Blackstone?"

Blackstone moved his head; affirmative or negative according to what you wanted.

"I see." Birnie made some notes. "That clears that up then. Now what about the matter of Sir Humphrey Cadogan? I gather that this informant of yours. . . . What's his name?"

"Lawler," Blackstone told him. The name as slippery and easy to forget as its owner.

216

"I gather this man."—the name immediately eluding him—"discovered that it was Cadogan himself who started the betting spree on the Bristol butcher. I won't ask how he found out. . . ." He waited. "It's none of my business, I suppose . . ."

Blackstone finished his tea, coughing as the smoke from the coal fire and Birnie's pipe entered his lungs.

"Very well," Birnie said. "I won't pursue that. But why did Cadogan do it? To pay the blackmailers?"

"Perhaps. Not necessarily. I've found out that he was penniless. Gambling debts mostly. He owed Gully the bookmaker a small fortune and had promised to pay him after the fight."

"And this man Donnelly?"

"He was Cadogan's accomplice."

Blackstone thought: and everything was going smoothly for them both until I insisted on taking over Ebony's training. And might have continued going smoothly if Donnelly had succeeded in killing me in the snow that night.

"And now Donnelly's dead. Of natural causes?"

"Of natural causes," Blackstone confirmed.

"In a cellar in St. Giles."

"Yes, sir."

"With Edmund Blackstone in attendance."

Birnie walked to the window. Outside, a woman with a child in her arms was singing ballads.

Birnie said, "I hear they've got a ballad out about yesterday's fight already."

"They print them very quickly these days."

"What were you doing in that cellar, Blackstone?"

"Waiting for Donnelly, sir."

Birnie sighed. "I feel I should ask you more. But it's never been my habit to go too deeply into the methods employed by the Runners. But it would be useful to have as much information as possible when I appear before these damned parliamentary committees." He looked hopefully at Blackstone.

"I was acting on information," Blackstone said. "I planned to apprehend him."

Irritation rasped Birnie's voice, Scots accent sharper when he was angry. "You're not in court now, Blackstone."

"I'm sorry, sir. But I don't think Donnelly need bother us too much. The coroner will record that he died from natural causes. From a visitation of God," he added, although this seemed unlikely in Donnelly's case.

Birnie said, "There doesn't seem to be much we can do about Cadogan. He hasn't committed an offense. And we are still looking for blackmailers."

"I don't think they have much hold over him now," Blackstone said. "The disgrace of an affair with one of his fallen women is nothing compared with the disgrace of a gentleman unable to pay his debts. His name will be posted in Tattersalls. In fact, Sir Humphrey Cadogan is ruined"

"We can't give up. A man was murdered."

"Ah, yes," Blackstone murmured. "King Rat."

"Because he had in his possession an incriminating letter?"

"Not exactly," Blackstone said.

"More to it than that?"

Blackstone nodded. "I'm afraid so, sir."

"Why afraid?"

Blackstone said, "I'd rather answer your questions tomorrow, sir, if you don't mind."

"I do mind," Birnie said. "But I suppose I can't do much about it."

"I could be wrong. I wouldn't want to make a fool of myself."

"No," Birnie said, "that would never do."

Lawler was waiting in a corner of the Brown Bear. Blackstone paid him for services rendered and bought two pots of ale.

The serving girl said, "I see you're in print, Mr. Blackstone." She handed him the halfpenny ballad sheet headed "Blackstone's Fancy" recording the scenes at Epsom Downs.

"Why don't you sing it?" Blackstone asked.

She looked at him closely and said, "You look very tired. Been having some exhausting nights?"

"One or two," Blackstone said with a flippancy that he didn't feel.

"You want to watch that, Mr. Blackstone," Lawler said as the girl walked away. "She means business."

"And you want to mind your own business," Blackstone said.

"You're pleased with me, aren't you, Mr. Blackstone?"

"I'm pleased. And you've been paid. Handsomely."

Lawler shook his head. "You're a hard man, Mr. Blackstone."

"I know," Blackstone said.

"There's the matter of expenses ..."

Blackstone looked at the list Lawler had prepared. "Which screever drew this up for you?"

"A man I know."

"How old are you, Lawler?"

"About thirty," Lawler said. "I think."

Blackstone said, "The screever seems to have added your age on to the total." He ordered two more pots of ale. "I'll give you half."

Lawler took the money and left.

Maisie was waiting outside. "Did you get it?" she asked.

Lawler nodded, stopping a hackney carriage.

"What's the hackney for, Lawler?"

"For you," he said. "You've got style, Maisie. You should always travel in hackneys."

"Just me?" she asked.

"Just you," Lawler said. He gave her half the money.

"Where are you going, Lawler?"

"Home," he said. "I'm not much of a hand at putting the cat out."

Maisie started to reply but he was walking rapidly away in the direction of the Rookery.

18

The household waited with mixed feelings for Sir Humphrey Cadogan to shoot himself. A few servants hoped that he would show the strength of will to live with his disgrace, recalling what good wages he paid; the others said it didn't matter one way or the other because he wouldn't be able to pay them. Sir Humphrey elected to live with his disgrace.

Daffodils swayed in the garden and there were clouds of pink blossom in the trees when Blackstone arrived at Barnet to see Laura, who was spending a weekend at the mansion. The foliage dripped and the sun blinked between the showers which already had an April quality about them. The house with its blue-lidded windows looked entirely dependable, built above vaults of honor and unquestioned credit.

Sir Humphrey had locked himself in the library with several fathoms of claret on tap. The fallen women and the pugilists had departed by that morning's mail. A maid was beating carpets in the yard.

Blackstone took the Poacher to the stables where a groom was brushing one of Cadogan's horses.

The groom said, "What are we going to do, Mr. Blackstone?"

"You'll get another position," Blackstone told him without conviction; glimpsing again the attendant tragedies of one man's downfall.

"It's not that easy, Mr. Blackstone."

"I'll see what I can do," Blackstone said vaguely.

In the hall the housemaid also expressed anxiety.

"I'll see what I can do," Blackstone told her too.

He kissed Laura on the scar. Her face was pale but there was an air about her suggesting that she wasn't heartbroken by her father's downfall.

Blackstone said, "Can we go somewhere private? We've a lot to talk about."

"Have we?" The sexually emancipated Laura Cadogan smiled. "We can go to your room. Or mine for that matter."

"The gymnasium, perhaps?"

"I hate that place."

"It's empty now," Blackstone said. He took her arm.

She sat on a chair in the changing-room, distaste lodged on her face.

Blackstone paced around for a while, staring through the window at the burgeoning garden.

Finally he said, "I know everything, Laura."

"About what?"

"You see," he said, words as careful as a guilty witness's, "I spoke to Amy Lawson last time I was here."

"I don't understand. . . ."

222

"The other girl, Ethel, confided in Amy."

Laura looked as arrogant as she had the day he arrived at the mansion, emotion contained beneath taut celestial blue.

"You'll have to explain yourself better than this," she said.

He fondled the gold snuff-box, his pacifier. "If it will make it any easier, we both lied."

"I know you did," she said.

Blackstone was startled. "In what way?"

"That you were involved in all this." She gestured around the gymnasium.

"How did you know that?"

"Donnelly told me. He hated you, that man," she said. "He would have done anything to hurt you."

"He did," Blackstone said. "He tried to kill me." A twig scratched the window, beckoning. It was very cold in the gymnasium. "I suppose I've known for a long time," Blackstone went on. "Without admitting it to myself."

She remained silent.

"The first indication was the wording of the letter threatening your father. I knew it was composed by a screever. But no screever that I know of is so addicted to the word *depravity*. Poor old screever," he added. "Poor old King Rat."

"I think," she said, "that I should leave."

"I think you should stay."

She stood up and, gently, he made her sit down again.

"I'll call for help."

"Do so. Although it's doubtful if anyone would interfere with a Bow Street Runner questioning a suspect."

"A suspect? Suspected of what?"

"Murder," Blackstone said.

She laughed and for the first time Blackstone heard the madness. He hurried on:

"You hated your father. With good reason. You hated him for what he did to you when you were a girl; for his brutality. You hated him for his hypocrisy with these women." Blackstone pointed towards their quarters.

"I hated him," she said, smiling. "Oh yes, I hated him all right. I still do. . . ."

"So you decided to embark on some good works yourself. Very commendable. But the noble charity you joined wanted money. Right, Laura?"

"Charities always want money."

"I wonder how much of that money finds its way to The Cause."

"Why don't you make that your next assignment?"

"Perhaps I will. Anyway you decided that the time had come to revenge yourself on your father and raise some money at the same time. Just about this time Lily Spender turned up abusing your father and threatening him." And now a little guesswork, Blackstone thought. "You got to know about this—overheard her, probably . . ."

He waited but Laura didn't interrupt.

". . . Poor Lily didn't realize quite what a danger she represented to your father. But you did, didn't you, Laura? You paid off Lily. Twenty pounds, was it? A considerable sum for Lily. And she parted with the letter your father had written to her." Blackstone sat down in front of Laura. "A disgusting letter, wasn't it, Laura?"

She nodded, lips trembling, scar screwed up.

"But it's not easy for a girl like yourself to get things done in London's underworld. Beautiful society girls are not advised to enter ratting taverns in Soho even if they do

224

represent reform and charity. So you took Ethel into your confidence. She knew her underworld all right, her screevers, her thimble riggers . . ."

"Perhaps," Blackstone acknowledged, "you didn't know the profession of the man Ethel hired. My watchdog, the murderer. But he won't be difficult to find—even if he trims his thumbnail."

Laura leaned forward. "Go on," she said in her slightly slurred voice.

"Ethel got the screever and you met him away from the Soho tavern. Depravity . . . an expressive word. You then delivered the letter and waited for your father, savior of fallen women, to pay up. Instead of that he called me in."

"I fell in love with you that day," Laura said.

"You have an unusual way of expressing love."

"No," she said. "I didn't do anything to hurt you. If you think about it you'll see that's true. I even went on loving you when I found out about the fighting . . . I think I sensed that you were doing it for the sake of the black boy."

Blackstone took some snuff. The twig scratched, its leaves polished with warm light. In the gymnasium it had grown colder. "You murdered a man," he said.

"No."

Blackstone said, "Apart from Ebony the only person who knew I was going to see the screever that day was you. I sent him to you with the message. Remember? So it had to be you. I checked up and found that Ethel was also in London that day supposedly being interviewed for a post in service—in other words Sir Humphrey had grown tired of her juvenile appeal. King Rat . . ."

"King Rat?"

"The screever, the forger. He had to be stopped from

telling me the whole story. So you told Ethel and she got in touch with our friend the thimble rigger. Luckily for you Shoemark decided to delay me by pretending he had the letter from Sir Humphrey. The delay was longer than he anticipated because when I next saw him he was dead."

"I didn't want him to be killed," Laura said.

"No," Blackstone said. "But that doesn't alter anything."

"What happens now?"

"I shall have to take you to London."

"Now?"

"No," he said. "In the morning. We'll take the mail."

"Did you love me?"

"Yes," he said, leaving her with something.

"I'm glad," she said.

She kissed him and was gone. Door swinging, warm spring air taking the chill from the place.

Blackstone put away his snuff-box and posted the groom outside Laura's room.

"Laudanum," the doctor said next morning. "No doubt about it."

Blackstone looked down at Laura's cold peaceful features. "At least she had more courage than her father," he said.

"What do you mean by that? We mustn't presume . . ."

"I'm not presuming anything," Blackstone said. He bent over the bed, "But you did have more courage . . ."

He kissed the scar and left.

EPILOGUE

Shortly after this period prizefighting went into a decline. Its corruption was too blatant: its exponents more interested in *crossing* fights than promoting them. This was lethal ammunition for the opponents of the prize-ring. In 1824 Jem Burns and Ned Neale fought at Moulsey. A prosecution followed at Kingston Assizes and Mr. Justice Burrough ruled that prizefighting was against the law. Moulsey ceased to be an arena for milling; the rich patrons had already largely withdrawn their support. Prizefighting did continue and new rules of fair-play were introduced. But it never really regained the seedy excitement of its Georgian heyday.